JUANITA WILDROSE
My True Life

JUANITA WILDROSE
My True Life

Susan Downe

PEDLAR PRESS | ST JOHN'S

ACKNOWLEDGEMENTS
The publisher wishes to thank the Canada Council for the Arts and the NL Publishers Assistance Program for their generous support of our publishing program..

LIBRARY AND ARCHIVES CANADA
CATALOGUING IN PUBLICATION

Downe, Susan, 1932-, author
    Juanita Wildrose : my true life / Susan Downe.

ISBN 978-1-897141-58-8 (pbk.)

    I. Title.

PS8557.O8295J83 2013   C813'.54   C2013-903179-0

EDITORIAL SUPPORT Maleea Acker

COVER PHOTO From the Estate of Juanita Emack Thompson

DESIGN Zab Design & Typography, Toronto

TYPEFACE Dolly

PRINTED IN CANADA

JUANITA WILDROSE
My True Life

...let the rose bloom
every year for her.
For this is Orpheus:
metamorphosis into one thing,
then another.
— RILKE, 1875-1926

What a mother brings
            through darkness still
to her parched daughter

— CAROL ANN DUFFY, "Water"

PART ONE

*

There were sins.

They came back, hurtling, remorseless.

Mom thought of them as *pentimenti*, events she painted over those many years ago, surfacing now.

At first they came in dreams, and she woke up knowing that the dreams were true representations of her omissions and commissions, how she hurt her children. Soon they came by day as intact memories. In the end, they were a cacophony of sounds and sights. She said, "They emboss me."

She had insight. She told her children, grown now, that her harshness had been an outcome of fear that she would not be a good mother; she must be vigilant, shape her children to the ideals that dwelled in her imagination. Her anguish was relentless. She reviewed, she reviewed. My reply each time was that she had done the best she could, I had no doubt of it, and, one day, exasperated, I said, "Look at us! We turned out fine!" None of our forgiveness, our reassurances, made enough difference; she continued to suffer.

One day I felt as she felt, remembering my similar failures. I told her and she felt the truth in me. She understood that I knew her torment in myself.

That was the beginning of the end of her suffering. It was also the beginning of her days as a sweet woman.

We had years in which to know her all over again: how she was before.

Once we've got our seatbelts on and we're on our way down the Varna Road, I say, Mom, we've got to do something about that big pile of brush out in the meadow. It's getting huge. I know, she says, we're going to have to burn it. Well, I say, we thought to last year, but one of us said John won't like it because all that smoke will thin the layer of upper ozone, or add to the lower ozone, whichever one, and so we didn't set fire to it. Then Mom and I say together, But we have to get rid of it somehow, and she says, I worry about polluting, too. I even think that maybe I shouldn't get cremated because it's not good for the environment, all that smoke, and then when I'm in the ground, I'll leach into the water table. Mom, I say, if you leach out of the cemetery in Bayfield, you're going to get into that underground stream that comes straight west and you're going to wind up in the basement of your own house. And we both laugh because it's true, the basement floods all the time from that ground water. And, I say, we'll just sump-pump you out into the grass in the east lawn. And she laughs and says, You'll never get rid of me.

Then she tells me she's been thinking about an urn for her ashes, and there are two vases she got at auction sales that are on the glass shelves in the bay window in the library, and those would be good to use if we could find some way to seal them. I say, Crazy glue, and tell her for the first time, that's what the funeral director suggested for the ashes of my sister, to keep the lid on the pot her friend had made for her, and how crazy Crazy glue sounded in that circumstance, but then, all the circumstances – that she died, even – felt crazy. And Mom says, That sounds like a good idea. And then she says, Maybe we could use that two-part vegetable dish we used today at lunch, and I say, That's great, one side for you and one side for Daddy, and she says, Maybe we couldn't stand to be so close for so long, but we have so far, and she remembers that this dish was a wedding present to her other daughter, my sister still alive, but she didn't like it and left it at Mom's house, and, Mom digresses, It's been so very useful. We fall silent, each thinking of those women, those lives. And ours, some. And dying.

We turn at Varna to drive south through the pale fields of corn, rattling papery in the wind. Beyond, great northern beans stretch deep yellow, even gold, in the westering sun. Mom pats my hand.

*

Dad is in the back seat, gazing blue-eyed out the side window; he lets the fields and woodlots and farmhouses flow by, his mouth at rest and smiling. He used to be the one to drive home. Today he sits quietly, hands peaceful in his lap. He wears a sky-blue *guyabera* (open at the neck, one of several – white, cream, blue – that he and Mom bought themselves during the Jamaica and Trinidad years) and a light-coloured straw hat with a black band. Its brim is bent awry, and is unfashionably narrow. Dad is famous in the family for his large head; all hats look too small on him, and fashion is of no concern.

My mother and I do not include him in our talk; deafness encloses him as if he is in another room. But I'm pretty sure I know his thoughts: "Huron County is the most beautiful part of the world; I never get tired of this trip – it's different every day of the year." He'll be remembering how Boz, Juanita's cousin and an agriculturist, was wowed by this countryside, couldn't get over the contrasts – the lushness of the land, the modesty of the houses. "You don't see that in the U.S. of A.!" We pass one of those houses, a yellow brick close to the road. In my mind's ear I hear Dad's voice reading the sign out front – Kathy's Kuts and Kurls – and he's laughing.

We will be home in an hour. I will pull into their driveway and Mom will say, "Jiggedy-jig," short for a verse about going to market to buy a fat pig and getting back home again. I'll turn off the ignition and Dad will say, "You're a good driver, Susie," and I'll think again a thought I've had lately: Here we are, three, Mom, Dad and me, as it was at my start, before the other kids, when all the days were agile, safe and free. When Mummy and Daddy sat up front in the black Dodge touring car, open to the sky and the breezes it made (a running board and a little folding gate on the side), when Daddy, before he started the engine, would extend his right arm along the top of the front seat, turn around and say, "Sit down, Susie, I don't want you falling out."

Charlie and I stomp our boots when we reach the porch, holler hellos as we enter, kick off our boots and hang up coats and scarves. Dad is in the study on the loveseat, supported by extra pillows, green and red. We bend to greet him.

"My favourite son-in-law named Charlie!" "My favourite daughter named Susan!" "My favourite grandson named Bret!" Everybody is royalty.

Chocolates on the table. Someone has brought lilies. Mom comes in from the kitchen with the celadon Wedgewood plates and Aunt Edith's forks, and lays them on the table. I go to the kitchen to whip cream. My brother follows, and pokes little pastel candles into the cake, makes the shape of an 8 and then a 7. We huddle to light them, then proceed back to the study. As we reach the doorway, everybody starts to sing. Dad pretends a modest surprise, then, not pretending, looks pleased with the cake, magical in light. Wish. Blow. Cheers.

This birthday is like Dad's other birthdays. We sit in the little green study after the McNeil/Lehrer News Hour and eat orange cake made from Mom's recipe from Kate Reid, and drink the coffee Ana and John have brought in black thermoses, because Mom serves only instant.

Dad produces Peter Rechnitzer's annual letter. Peter is Dad's physician, now retired, and this year's birthday letter urges once again that Dad and Peter go into business together to manufacture and market Substance 80, which will make them both rich. Peter is confident that there is a huge market out there for Dad's qualities and attitudes, which they will distill into an Essence. Dad says it's time to start thinking about Substance 90.

Mom sits beside Dad and pats his hand. I think about Dad's bewilderment at his frailness. A while back, he asked Peter point-blank, "Just exactly what is the matter with me?" Peter replied, "Dr. Thompson, you've got a bad case of the Eighties."

Charlie pours coffee into our cups. John asks about other birthdays. "On your birthday, did Grandma cook you special food, things you especially liked?" Dad pauses, says, "Nope."

We wait. He continues. "Everything Momma cooked was special. All her dishes were favourites."

The side of Mom's refrigerator is plastered with two-inch lengths
of masking tape, each one lettered in black magic marker. The
tapes are placed more or less horizontally and I can read them just
by glancing over. They are, to judge by their various shades of ecru
and ochre and white, of widely varying ages. I read them every time
I dry dishes while Mom washes. The whole side of the fridge and its
mosaic of cryptic marks look, I say, "like notices pasted on a public
wall in Beijing: '2 c. blk. Bn. Sp.' '2½ c. sw. st. rhbb.'" Meanwhile,
Mom is remembering out loud, "...When Daddy was invited to the
Explorers' Club, the invitation was for medals or native dress..."

'Marie's ham – 3"'

'½ lb. glc. ssge'

"...and Daddy of course had neither this nor the other, although his
native dress might have been overalls and garden boots..."

"And his beat-up Panama hat," I say.

"...Yes, and he would have caused a stir right there on Central Park
West. But he just wore his regular navy-blue suit, so when he went
in the very imposing front door, Cousin Boz – who met him in the
hall – took him over to a freckle-faced woman seated at a little table.
She opened a drawer and took out a medal, and handed it to Daddy,
and Boz pinned it on Daddy's lapel, 'For your wounds,' Boz said, and
they walked on in to dinner."

Mom racks her memory. "I don't know what kind of medal it was.
Do you suppose a Purple Heart?"

I veer. "Mom, what's this? I've been looking at it for about five years: '2 Tbsp. fg jm'."

Mom shakes soapy water from her hands and steps over. "Where? Oh. That's fig jam. Two tablespoons of fig jam. It's the label for the next time I need to put away two tablespoons of fig jam in the fridge or freezer."

"Mom!"

"I know."

I peel the fig tape from the fridge and turn to paste it (stickiness almost gone) to Mom's apron front – a medal: "There, Mom, a fig for she who..."

Mom takes her magnifier from her breast pocket and brings her face close to peer. "Let's find one for you."

Tuesday morning again. I call for the list. Mom has it in her hand as she lifts the phone. She takes a moment to retrieve the magnifying glass from her breast pocket.

"Now," she says: "Graham crackers, only they're not. You know the kind I mean." (She means Wasa.)

"Digestives. With no chocolate."

"*Ice-a cream.*" (The customary Italian accent.)

"Baby food. Prunes and meats." (For Dad.)

"The applesauce you got on sale has run out. Applesauce."

"Wheat bran."

"Big Kleenex. Little Kleenex."

"More paper things. You should see the way we use paper towels around this place. Paper towels."

"Razors for Daddy."

"What else? Bananas. We have three left. Four or five."

"No celery this time. Lettuce."

"Dry milk. Wet milk."

(When she dies, will I be able to get into the bed to hold her?)

"The nurse wants that special lotion you got for Daddy last time. You got it at Big V. That's all. I think. What else? Light bulbs."

"Oh – 'malted wool.' What do you suppose *that* is? I'll put down the phone so I'll have two hands to hold the magnifier up – just a minute."

"Mouthwash!"

*

HOW LARGE my father's feet are
now that he is small.
My mother sits to face him, his thighs
as slim as ivory, she strokes
their skin, she milks
them with her joyful, urgent hands

  and all the bones and feathers that I am
  fall out of this
  and all
  my sons and grandsons spun from this
  and no one knows the numbers

of caresses that remain.
How full they are!
These two, their faces
light as after making love
as leaves
shine after rain.

GETTING READY (JOY)

She is preparing me.

"How are you, Ma?" She has been very tired.

"Oh...fat - ee - gew, emphasis on fat. I'm getting fatter and shorter."

We talk about clothes that will fit for the hot weather. None of her sleeveless blouses will button up. Shall we take out the sleeves of some roomier blouses? Some of mine? I have not been able to find, in stores, blouses with two breast pockets. She wants them for modesty's sake, since underwear in the summer is too hot.

We seem to be stymied about this, but we know not to rush decision-making. One thing is clear. "I can't spend money on new clothes for me at this stage."

*

"*Four* cans?" (I've brought four cans of Heinz vegetable cocktail, 48 oz. each.) "I'll be dead long before these are gone." She is getting used to the idea of being gone. A difficult thing to think about.

*

She is fearless.

"The other night when I had the pressure in my chest, like a huge green fist, I had the thought, 'I am going to die now.'"

Her fingers make little flowers in the air.

"And, this is the thing. I was filled with joy."

She lifts her arms. "I just felt myself lifted up. Then I thought, but how could I have forgotten even for a moment? I cannot leave Walter. Then the pressure got very bad."

The quiet between us is lush and snowy. She begins again, "I wanted to tell you...it is like they said, '...and He was lifted up.' In the Bible. And Jacob, his ladder...up into the sky. It really is like that. Perhaps everyone knows this. But the ones who die cannot tell us. And the ones who live don't tell it. I was filled with joy! I thought I was going to die, and I was *filled* with joy."

IN MCGILLIVRAY TOWNSHIP'S
CHERRY TREES

birds enraptured by ripeness
hurtle into the waiting nets
and the summer men in leather gloves
pluck them out
and drown them quick in buckets

My father, thin and asleep
in his cotton sling, arcs
over the width of his bed
lifted and swung by an hydraulic arm

tomorrow his eyes will stop.
Death is quick – the moment
between this and this
we cannot catch

WARM HANDS

expect warm hands
reason reports
his hands are cold
but my hands
don't believe it

I keep them there, shocked children,
against their will

until they know

*

We could call him back!
His hands
his cheeks
are chill –
but his chest!
his chest and the top of his glorious head
– *warm.*

*

Under his ribs his heart
still sends forth heat
I rest my ear
and my naked cheek
on his chest

Praise still *pours*

was St. Patrick's Day, the day
we used to plant potatoes on the farm, when I
was a child, the day I learned to read a word.

The day we met
was ordinary in the morning, though I'd cut
my hair the day before, the century almost
twenty-two and I was seventeen, the War
was three years over.
            The day we met
Miss Craig had marked me a hundred and one on
my essay on *Twelfth Night*. The night before
I'd eaten Campbell's soup like always, slept
like always, started to learn the *Canterbury
Tales* by heart, *whan that Aprille with his showres
soote the droughte of March hath percèd to the roote*

and the day we met
he percèd me with the sweetest smile I ever saw I never
saw another like it, saw him in a doorway at a party
on St. Patrick's Day, I never deviated after that.

*

I have heard the story all my life. This time I write it down.

She says, "I can see him and his sweet smile as if it is right now. So
clearly. Isn't it strange that I am blind, and yet I see so clearly."

The Fence

Husband, where you are
the sloping field
lies far and green in sun
and you inside O

can you see me?

The Road

Where the road I remember
from the farm
forks east north west
strong men labour
            barricaded
in their fate

they bend without a murmur
over shovels, picks
their task – to mend again.

Two Ramps

Walk on ahead
while I go back
to get the makings for our meal
      Take
the left-hand slope
green as home
and when I come
I'll climb the other one.

The Top

I thought it would be you
here at the top
but what I was certain was you
is an empty coat.

Dresses

I take apart
my dresses – each one
was sewn of panels
three in front
(the centre panel split)
and three in back
a collar Yes

     the work

is hard

to stitch them back together
each to each
exchanging panels apple-
green and patterns sprigs
of periwinkle little rosy moons
but now each dress is a dress
of many dresses

     and I
     am satisfied.

Stirring

(How did I not see you
when I came in?)
you're stirring something
at the stove

you shining
smile at me   O
    face   O

sun more than the sun is

porridge!
For our breakfast

Servings get smaller and smaller. "By the time I reach my birthday, I'll be eating less than a bird; I'll be down to a teaspoon." She pictures herself at the kitchen window, opening wide its two doors, and handing the spoonful out to a sparrow, holding the spoon still while the soft grey-brown thing pecks and swallows and polishes off the – what? (not her chopped salad) – a spoonful of bulgur. "Birds and I like bulgur."

Lunch actually looks good. She's cut a slice of John's bread in half. The bread is bursting with good things – flours and seeds – and she's spread it with ricotta cheese, laid that on her plate beside the salad. Salad in wintertime is so pale, scarcely green at all, bereft of the colours and flavours of parsley and tarragon and lovage and mint and those fragrant things.

"Still, after a while you don't miss what you don't have. This tastes good. Except Walter. With him, I do miss what I don't have." The dream comes back.

"I'm back again at the same place, broad and square, like the farm at home, a section. The terrain is similar and it's different. Here in my dream the farm's sloping hill is a cliff; below, where the creek was, is a low hill, and high and low, where in my dreams there are almost always wildflowers, today there are none. The limbs of the hickories are bare. Underfoot lie all their fallen leaves, thick, thick on the ground. Walter has been walking beside me until now, but now I cannot find him. I cannot find him. Then I am sure he is under the leaves. I need him back! And I cannot find exactly where he is. I run off to the right, I try to catch the attention of workmen to come and help. Help me find Walter! But I cannot catch their attention. I return to the leaves. This time, it feels good that Walter is there, under the leaves."

*

We walk up the ramp on the side of the house. Mom stops partway. "I'm gettin' old."

"You've got a youthful spirit."

"I need it. You need it more when you're old than when you're young. When you're young, you're just busy trying to grow up. Now I've grown up – and guess what? I'm old."

*

"The big job of the day, of course, is doing my toenails."

All the clocks are breaking down. When I come into the kitchen, five are lined up on the counter.

"Ominous, don't you think?" says Mom.

"It is amazing. But…think of light bulbs. If you put them all in at once, they all blow at once. When did you buy…?"

"I did buy these two at the same time. But the others…And this one – it's battery operated. I put in a new battery. Nothing."

She hands me a plastic bag wrapped with a rubber band. It contains half a dozen warranties for clocks. These, I think, could go into a museum. "I'll go to Wallace's," I say, "and get a new clock."

"Ninety years without slumbering," she sings, "tick-tock, tick-tock." Then, "Never mind. I can move the upstairs electric clock to my side of the bed. I've got an extension cord. You can help me with it. But get me a new oven timer. Can you believe it? We bought this in '94 and it's broken."

*

She has a stack of notes, inches thick, of things she's been thinking about, things she does not want to forget. This is today's:

Book of Job

John Jim Jeremy (these are nephews)

Jocasta

Indonesia

Mary Barker

Order of Canada (box)

"Let's not go back to Mark Twain's letters today. Read me the chapter about the earliest years at the Biz School. When Ellsworth – no, Ellis – Morrow was first there. Did you know that Dr. Fox was educated in Geneva and at Johns Hopkins? Classics. And before he came here, he taught at Princeton for a while."

*

"When I first went to Springfield, to Jefferson Avenue, away from home and Mama and Papa, I sometimes envisioned them in mid-air, like angels. They were wearing their work clothes, and they were looking down at me."

*

"Did I tell you that two of us had double-toes? Not six toes, but the two middle toes grown together. It was Mark, and Ruth, I think; wait! Maybe Elizabeth and maybe George. But it wasn't both Mark and Elizabeth. I would remember if it was both twins."

Mom is so bent today, and so weary. Her throat is sore and I worry; she's never sick. But we took her temperature and it registers normal.

My heart turns as she struggles to her feet and walks slowly (glad for the secure feel of her Nikes) to the living room. She doesn't need to remind me where she keeps the ancestors (our old way of putting it, 'the ancestors' the name left over from when we were all children at home). It's a collection of photographs and letters and copies of letters and, in his own hand, Mom's father's graduation essay, "Race Education," from high school.

The upper, left-hand drawer of Mom's desk. It's the letters I want – to Locust Grove, from James William and George Malcolm, Richmond, 1862. Dear Mother. Dear Sister.

"Your cousin Rosalie has most of them. Mama gave them to her, the original letters, a long time ago – I think because she pitied her, who had nobody on her father's side, including a father. I wish we had those letters now."

"I'll write Rosalie, ask her to send copies."

Mom doesn't hold out much hope. "Rosalie is ungiving."

I take the letters Mom has. "I'll take these home and read them onto tape. Then you can listen whenever you want to."

She looks glad. I have an idea to ask my son to read them instead so they'll, appropriately, be in a young man's voice.

"Is he a good reader?"

"There are a few things I forgot to mention until now. Just so you know – in case you don't already – Aunt Nannie was bossy and unreasonable. Oh, never mind that. What I mean to say is she made me wear a corset. A corset! I had nothing up front, and nothing behind, and I was to wear a corset."

"Make sure to wash your crystal at least once a year; even if you aren't using it, wash it or it dries out and becomes brittle. Especially Margaret Turner's little wine glasses, wash those."

"And Harry Lane's wife – so kind to help me at Jack Wettlaufer's funeral, do you recall what a storm it was that day? And everyone crowded around Daddy because he couldn't walk, and I couldn't see, and she helped me to the car. Don't forget her and Harry, make sure they're on the list to be invited to the garden dedication. Also, David Suzuki. Don Kishibe's cousin. John will have his address."

*

It's two weeks to the dedication party. Two hundred people have written they're coming, and more will at the last minute. The School has planted a small vegetable plot with one row of corn, two of tomatoes and three of cucumber plants, these in remembrance of all the vegetables Dad used to bring to school when there were floods of them in the garden. The darling young people who are planners for this celebration, but who never knew Dad, have caught some of the goodness Dad was, and are deeply connected to the event. We will plant fifty daffodils from the yard at Bayfield. The bronze plaque with the bas-relief of Dad's head will be a good-enough likeness, I hope.

*

I am afraid that her body under the coverlet all over with wildflowers will be too small. But she makes a substantial shape, full of breath. I touch her shoulder and she jumps.

"Did I scare you?"

"You didn't scare me; you surprised me." Precise: a good sign. Her hands are warm. She holds mine.

"Your hands feel cold." Then, "I am shivery." Rueful. "Just one more thing. It's as if I'll do anything to get attention. Like Christopher Robin."

We laugh (hers is faint, but definitely a laugh) about *Now how to amuse them today. Measles and tweezles*, and we ramble off into measles, and how catching them used to be so dangerous, and I tell her, for she has forgotten, that little children nowadays are inoculated against measles, and she says, "What a good thing."

"When I was little on Grosvenor Street," I remind her, "you kept my bedroom dark when I caught the measles, and wouldn't let me read, no matter how I begged. To save my eyes." I start to say, "So I wouldn't go blind," but don't, although that was the way she explained the no reading to me at the time.

"I don't remember that."

*

"Papa borrowed one thousand dollars when we got to Texas County, to buy a pair of horses and to build us a little house. It was a little shack, really, at first. The banker wouldn't let Papa pay it back in small amounts; he had to pay it back all at once. You can imagine how much interest that cost."

*

"For two winters, we were hungry. If it hadn't been for corn, we would have starved."

*

"You know how I am always wanting to look up and remember something in the Bible? It's as if, even now, I'm trying to catch up in knowledge to Mama. So we can converse together."

*

"Mama's conch was large, and blue-grey on the outside. At noon, she took it out to the porch, and blew Papa and the rest of us in for dinner."

*

"Mama and Papa held different views about sex. Mama thought you shouldn't unless you intended to have a child. Can you imagine how Papa felt about that?"

*

"When Papa died, Mama didn't want to live with Elizabeth yet. They made an arrangement so that Elizabeth would know every morning that Mama was all right. Mama ran the flag up her flagpole so Elizabeth, on the road over, could see it, and know all was well.

"Do you remember about Dr. Steely's son? He had spent years and years in prison for murdering someone when he was drunk. After Papa died, he came every evening and parked his car down the road from Mama's house. He slept there all night; it was so she'd be safe.

"I don't know what good that would have done if she had fallen or had a heart attack, but that's what he did."

"The Mirrills had water, and so probably were more sanitary than most. They had a big L-shaped porch off the back of their house, and in the small arm of the L was a pump that pumped up fresh water. They had a cistern too, and this meant they were able to catch and keep the soft rainwater. Of course, that cistern got full of leaves, and they had to clean it out once a year.

"The Mirrills had two daughters. One was a wonderful schoolteacher, but she didn't teach at our school; she taught in another town, and they kept her there, she was so wonderful. And there was a son, a roué, and everybody knew he'd fathered a lot of children in the neighbourhood, children raised by husbands and by parents of single girls.

"In the hills on either side of us lived the Hunters and the Hales, Cherokees who survived the Long March. Others in the neighbourhood were Swedes and Norwegians, new to this country, and the Cooks, who came from England, though the second Mrs. Cook was a Skleiber, a Czech. These people married each other, and in some cases wives were second wives, the first ones having died, the life so hard. I think that's why some of us are long-lived, we're descendants of the survivors.

"Grandma Mirrill lived in a fine house. She slept in a bed in their living room, and upstairs were two small attic rooms, finished, not raw-ceilinged like most of us had. Mirrills had a good big kitchen and the big porch I told you about.

"Even though she didn't have any real relatives in the area, Mrs. Mirrill was 'Grandma' to everyone. What stands out in my memory is what Mr. Mirrill said a lot. "She's always got at least one clean finger," and this was a reference to the way she cooked."

PART TWO

...I saw

that I was a speck of light in the great
river of light that undulates through time.

I was floating with the whole
human family.

– JANE KENYON, "Once There Was Light"

Juanita | Mallie | Christine

Our family moved from Wichita, Kansas, to Texas County in Missouri, in 1906. Of course, when we left Wichita, our family was only Mama and Papa, Mary Christine and me. But when I think of us, it seems to me that Mama for certain and probably Papa too brought George and Mark and Ruth and Elizabeth along with us, clear in their minds to the last detail, even though they weren't born yet.

But George almost was. In fact, Mama could tell that George would be born on the way, at about the time we reached Webb City, so we stopped there for a while in a house Papa rented for us – long enough for George to be born and Mama to get her strength back.

Our old house in Wichita was wonderful, a big, white house on a city lot that ran down in back to the Gold River. I was little, but even if I'd been older and bigger, I know I would still have found our backyard mysterious as a forest, and beautiful. We didn't want to leave, but Papa's doctor told him his lungs were in trouble and he would die if he continued to work with the chemicals at the mine. He must go someplace where the air was clean. So Papa talked to a land broker, who said he would take our place in Wichita in exchange for a place in Texas County, Missouri, which would provide us with mountain air, clean water and a nice house.

We were on our way, and Webb City was for just a little while. "Webb City is an Encountering Place," said Mama. "It's where Papa and I met each other." Now it was the place where we would meet George, although we had met him through Mama's stomach muscles before, Mary Christine and I holding our ears close against her big front, feeling him move around and even kick.

The midwife came. George came out slippery and red and with wet hair and squalled to the world. When he gets big, we'll tell him about this day and he'll run because he won't want to hear about coming out "down there." Mary Christine and I will start to tell him that everybody does, but he'll holler No No and keep running.

*

"Where did you meet Papa?" asks Mary Christine.

"I'll tell you another time."

"Church," says Papa, "the Methodist Church. And me an Episcopalian." He slys his eyes to Mama.

She has a little curve on her mouth, but keeps on fastening George to her breast. Episcopalian?

"High Church of England," says Papa.

"England?" says Mary Christine.

By now we are on the train to Cabool. Papa says we may walk up to the end of the coach and back, being careful, holding onto the handles.

When we get off at Cabool, Papa loads us and our things from home onto a hired horse-and-cart. We follow the road alongside Elk Creek to the farm. Or, what should be the farm, but is not. Instead, it is stony land and there is no house. We walk around for a while. Someone has piled boulders in what was to have been our spring.

*

That is why we have moved into a house on this land near to ours. It is four walls, a grass roof and a floor of dirt packed down hard. Papa has to duck to get in; it is a short house. It is Mr. Fisher's place, empty, with a fence around it. Mr. Fisher is somewhere else. He left us an orchard a long way off, to take care of and to harvest. That is instead of paying rent. It is Papa's daily work, apart from clearing our land so we can plant a garden. After that, we will build a house.

*

All around this place is free range. Papa says it's called free range because nobody pays taxes on it, but I think it's because it's so far in every direction, out to the small line all around where the sky touches down, and beyond our woods not a tree, not a house anywhere. Clouds fly fast from one side of the world to the other, and so does the big wind, and even the word f r e e sounds like wind in the grass, bowing and bending, so mostly "free range" means that kind of free.

And here is our house, right in the middle. Even with the big wind and the animals, there is a big quiet here.

The cattle come. Anybody's cattle can graze on free range. Those great slow animals make it their business to eat their way all day north to south or south to north, always facing in the same direction as each other, as birds do flocking. They tear off swaths of grass as big as brooms with muscle-y, raspy tongues, and swallow whole, exactly the way Mama says not to.

Always we see when a herd is coming. At first it's like a thickening of the line where the sky touches the land, the outline, and over the length of the day that herd moves like a slow ship across the range. Sometimes it comes close enough to the house that we can count the animals by their backs and their nodding, circling heads. Of course, we could never count them all.

George went out to the fence one day to count, and then he started talking. They wouldn't listen at first, but then one, then maybe five, and then maybe a hundred, they all looked up and walked over to look at George, and George had never been so looked-at, and George looked them back. Hundreds of brown eyes with eyelashes looking at George and two blue eyes of George looking at them, and *nobody* talking.

After a long time, one of the big creatures stirred; then they all turned and followed away. George felt the hugeness of the walking-away and after, the bigness that was gone.

A few afternoons after George talked to the cattle, we hear a thunder. Christine and I are out in the dirt in front of the house, playing. Papa isn't home because he is hired out as an extra hand. Then we hear a thunder that does not stop. Mama all of a sudden pops out the door, keeping her hand on the latch. She makes a sound like a growl. "Girls, come in!" Mama never sounds like this. I always do what she says, but slower. This time fast. We pick up the jacks and walk fast into the house. Mama shuts the door hard, and slides the bolt across. Then she runs to the other door and does the same. She pushes the table over in front of that door.

It is everywhere now, the thunder. It fills our ears, and our feet can feel pounding right through the floor. The house begins to shake. We look around the room at everything rocking, and Mama quietly asks us to please put the dishes under the covers on the big bed. Mary Christine and I hold hands and strain our eyes toward the window. What is it?

A whole drove of cattle, running, running, an ocean toward us, and now Mama speaks the word that it is: *stampede.* Now the great wave of sound is here, and all those animals, hundreds and hundreds, come in great rocking motions over our fence as if it isn't there at all. They come straight for our house.

Then the wave breaks; it breaks in two, two huge brown rivers rush to the west of us and to the east, and still they pour and pour. It lasts a long time. Then we can hear it ending. The last hundreds slow and come right up to our walls, and those that are at the windows look in at us. The thunder is over. Such a silence. Only a big silent pounding in our ears, only all that breathing.

Not ours. I think Mama and we children stopped breathing about the time the fence fell. We are standing like statues. Now we have to go look. It is the same out all the windows. Cattle right up to our walls. Then they leave, as they left from George that day; first one, then more, then the whole river of them. By the time Papa comes home, there is nothing but the story which we tell over and over, our fence squashed flat on the ground, and hoofprints, hoofprints, hoofprints.

40 acres, from 4 to 5 miles North East of Cabool Texas Co. Mo, on the Houston and Elk Creek Public road. Part valley or bottom land, all tillable land, all fenced with rail fence. About one half of this 40 acres is in cultivation the ballance in timber, Line runs up to the Public Road. Good Spring, ¼ mile from School, ¾ mi from Church. One mile from Duvall Post Office. in a good neighborhood. Cabool is a splendid R.R. town on the Frisco R.O.R. Pop. about 1500.

Papa has built us a house on our land in the Valley, not so far from the Fisher Place. It is not big, but we are excited to move in. It is mostly one room and a kitchen attached, with a ladder to go up to where we children sleep. Mama says if I don't stop growing, she doesn't know where she's going to put me. I am not worried; I know that Mama doesn't want me to stop growing.

Papa dug a hole in the kitchen floor, with a door that lifts up with a rope handle, and we will keep our winter food down there. We have Old Kate, who ploughs, sort of, and we have Old Nellie, who is a mother and a darling person of a horse.

It is tricky to tell about the water here. Here it is complicated, not like the Arkansas River in Wichita long ago where we lived on Gold Street. There, our backyard ran down sloping to the water, and that water was calm and dignified. A city river.

But Elk Creek is not dignified. It's wandery and skips hither and yon as if it is a person jumping side-to-side, as if it is a kid having fun. It comes to the farm from the east, down from that high land. That's scary over there because of the Hunters, and we are not allowed to go onto Hunters' land. Also, there are rattlesnakes and scorpions. I know the creek when it gets to us. It skips along, east to west, wiggling as it comes, and just as it reaches our west boundary, it quick heads north.

There is a bridge on the Cabool-Elk Creek Road, and the creek flows under, keeps heading north, then veers off west again until it reaches its relative, sort of a big-boy cousin of a river, Big Old Piney. He is a great rushing water. Before it reaches that place, some miles back, it has met up with Little Old Piney, and all that two-rivers water is raring, just raring.

On the north road, the Lewises live next to the Hunters and next to them the Hales, and on down the road the Mahlbergs, Schoenbergs, Carlsens, Watsons and Larsons. On the east road is our school, and one over from there the Penningtons and Amundsons live. On the road coming near us are the Vollmers, the Mirrills, the Fishers and another branch of the Hales we call the "good Hales," with twelve really nice children, and Mama allows us to know them. That Mrs. Hale had been a Miss Hunter. On the fourth side are the Steelys. He is a minister and Steely Chapel is there; we don't go there. The Steelys don't have little ones, only two grown sons. Mrs. Miller, too, she is a sister of Mrs. Mahlberg.

Before now, we have called the Hales and the Hunters and the Lewises 'Indians.' But "Shawnee," says Christine.

"Not Shawnee," says Papa, "Cherokee. Cherokee Nation, Smokey Mountain Cherokee Nation, now gone. Only the Hales know their other name from Georgia."

"The Eastern Tribes, the mountain tribes north of the river in Georgia," says Mama, "Chickasaw, Choktaw, Cherokee," she stops.

"Chattahoochee, Chatooga, Nacoochie," says Papa.

All of a sudden, it stops being a naming lesson. Mama and Papa are prodding and having a race with each other and not paying any attention to us at all. We are excited by this newness so strange.

"Chickamauga, Tugaloo, Etowah," cries Mama.

"Don't forget that 'Wichita' is theirs."

"And back east, their names are still there: 'Chattanooga, Tennessee.'"

"Tennessee – are you sure?"

"Yes, Mr. Emack, Tennessee; I'm sure."

"We cast them out of their homes."

We are horrified. "We made them leave home?"

"Not us, exactly," says Mama.

"Yes, us," says Papa. "First to prison camps. Then we made them walk west on a long, long march: north and west, then south and west. Federal soldiers guarded them to make sure."

We are quiet. Then George has a big question on his face. "The Hunter girl twin, Pearly – she has yellow hair. How can she be an Indian – ah – Cherokee?"

Papa tells us, "If her Mama has one drop of Cherokee blood in her, she is a Cherokee. Their way of life is matriarchal."

We pop out our ears. "Matriarchal?"

"That means the mamas are the boss. Like at our house." He sends fluty eyes to Mama, who pretends to be thinking of something else all of a sudden.

Papa returns. "The Hales and the Hunters. Their grandmas and grandpas didn't walk all the way. They dropped off around here and were left for dead. But, as we know, they lived."

We feel glad about that part.

We know that the doctor in Cabool will never get to our house on time; he is out in the buggy and his wife doesn't know where. So Mama spreads clean cloths on hers and Papa's bed. Between puffings and holding onto the door frame tight with both hands, she tells Papa what to do. We children are sent to the kitchen to crack black walnuts and stay there, no nonsense, until Papa says Come out.

But we watch anyway, after a minute.

Papa hasn't done this before, but Mama has. She climbs carefully onto the bed and props herself up on her elbows. Mama is not noisy, but she is now. Her groans and pushes are so big that our house feels too small. Mama never sweats, but she does now, and her face is red, and...NOW! she groans to Papa, and Papa catches, and here is a baby. And all over again Mama groans another huge time, and here is another one...and is there another one?

And now Mama is laugh-crying, and Papa's hair is down over his forehead and nose, and his sleeves shoved up to the tops of his arms, and he crouches down and looking concentrative and amazed. Mama starts pushing again – there is another one! But this one is not a baby; it's a big blob of blood.

Now Mama sits up and shows Papa how to hold them high, the twisty wet ropes that attach the babies to the blob. Are the ropes alive? They are moving like swallowing. Mama hands Papa string and he ties strings close to the little babies' bellies. And now he cuts the ropes with the shears.

The babies are lying on Mama's stomach, and they start crying, small high cries like rabbits when the owl catches them in the dark. Mama lifts up the first one, and this one is a girl, and the second one, and this one is a boy! and now Mama and Papa wrap them in flannel squares saved from when we big ones were babies. Mama lies down again and Papa snugs one baby on her bosom, and now the other one, and Mama looks glad and frazzled.

Papa is down on his knees beside the bed and his face is all soft.

NAMES (TWINS)

The twins have hair that is almost invisible. Mama says they are going to be real tows, and that means their hair will be white. That doesn't mean there's something wrong with them, like being very old, it means their hair will be brown or light brown by the time they go to school. Mary Christine and George and I were not tows; we were brown from the start.

The twins are Mark and Elizabeth. They both have blue eyes, and Mark is bigger than Elizabeth. George says that's because he's the boy. Mama says Maybe. Papa teases Mama about their names, that they don't rhyme.

In the Valley, there are a lot of twins. Most of them rhyme. Before our twins were born, Mama said if she had twins she would leave the County. And she surely would not name them rhyming.

The Mirrills are the worst rhymers; their oldest twins are Pearly and Early, Early born first, and the little boys are Alvin and Elvin. Mama rolls her eyes. I think Marcus is queer, which is Mark's real name. Marcus is for an Emperor of Rome, but the real thing, Mama says, is that he was a philosopher and a writer.

Teeley and Mr. Hunter are also the worst: Alonzo and Alphonzo, older than me, and Moscoe and Roscoe. Ola and Lola are the Millers' twins (their Mama is Ana, and her twin sister is Ida, Mama's friend).

"Elizabeth is after Papa's sister, and you, Juanita – I always loved your name – came from a book of Spanish stories. The wild rose is the most beautiful of all the flowers, and that's what I thought of when you were born."

I wish it was only Rose. Wildrose isn't really a name of a person; it's a plant. Juanita Wildrose is the strangest name in our family, and too fancy. (p.s. Aunt Mattie has twins, same as us: Victor and Helen, not rhyming.)

The man who owned Old Kate before us named her just Kate. Papa bought her at auction. Mama said we should have called her That Man's Problem; this was when we found out that the horses at auction are other people's castoffs. Papa started calling her Old Kate when he found out how mean she is. Papa takes her out to plough and she stands up on her back legs and rears and rears. It's because she hates to plough. Papa could get killed. But we keep her. Papa says he intends to keep *at* her until she gives in. Mama says Papa is more stubborn than Old Kate.

Old Nellie is the gentlest, our favourite horse. Mary Christine sits in the saddle, and I sit in front, and George sits behind, and she waits as still as still until we're all on, and then she begins to walk, very slowly.

Her children are Roxanne and Mera. Roxy is haughty and never wants to be ridden; "wild and willful" we call her. Mera isn't like that at all. When Papa said "It's a filly" when Mera was born, Mama gazed off the way she does, and then she told Papa, "her name is Mera."

THIS DAY, ST. PATRICK'S DAY, is special.

Not just because one saintly person got rid of a whole country-full of snakes, but because today we plant the potatoes. "That's what people do here," says Papa.

He harrows the big garden; Old Kate rears and rears because she hates the plough, Papa rassles her and makes her plough anyway, and after a whole day of it the garden is ready.

We are in the kitchen cutting up potatoes – seed potatoes, which we had to trade from Mr. and Mrs. Joliffe for corn because ours rotted and the mice got them, also voles and some other creature: Mama shudders to think. "I hope not rats."

Three eyes for each piece of potato. The eyes will grow. I hate this idea; I think of eyes coming out of the eye-holes of my face, on white stalks and reaching up and up when I'm buried, when my eyes want sun and the fresh air and start moving up from under the ground. Mama says, "Nonsense, that doesn't happen, ever."

She says it's not like that for potatoes either, and now she's making it up. "It's not the sun, it's the stars they reach for. When the small white potato flowers come up and unfold, there they are, stars in the sky and stars in the garden."

We plant the little three-eye pieces in rows and cover them with earth, only three inches; we'll heap more dirt on bit by bit as the stems and leaves come up. By harvest, each little potato piece equals eight whole big potatoes.

But this St. Patrick's Day is the most historic for two other reasons. First, Mary Christine tells Mama and Papa she doesn't want to be Mary anymore, she wants us to call her only Christine. And then, reading.

*

After supper, Mama reads out loud. We are in the middle of *David Copperfield*. I lean over Mama and look for letters. I have known the Ss for years. I know Ls and of course Ns and Ms, and Os, what they sound like, and Xs, which are hard to make a sound, and Ts.

Mama reads, and we children crowd in close on her bed and I look for letters. Mama holds her finger on a place on the page and lifts her head to say something, maybe explain, so I look where her finger is and see the S she's just said and some more words that have Ss, and all of a sudden I know a word – right here! My ears stop up. Mama keeps on reading and I try to find where she is but I can't – until she turns the page and now – it happens again – a word, the same word!

"SEE!" Mama and everybody stares at me and me saying, "Mama, right here – S - E - E, Mama, that says SEE."

George is too young to know what is wonderful, but Christine knows, and Mama calls, "Papa, come in here!"

And Papa comes in from the porch and I tell him, and he stands in the doorway holding his galluses and rises up on his toes and back down again and he smiles at me who can read now, and he says, "Well, Juanita."

It's not just their name; they really are hunters. Around here, the farmers are Norwegians, English, Germans and Swedes and us. Everyone thinks the Hunter men are shiftless because they don't plant a crop, but their tradition is that men are hunters; they go out from their falling-down houses with shotguns, and come home with small animals hanging from their hands: rabbits, groundhogs.

It means they are poor, poorer than us, because some days they shoot nothing, and also they have nothing to trade like we do – corn, eggs, cream.

Teeley Hunter comes to the door. Mrs. Emack, if you please, may we have flour? She asks as if it is a loan. But it is not. "She has her pride," Mama says, "like we do, except that we are brought up not to dissemble, no matter the situation. Plus, we work hard. We are not in a begging situation." Mama has a struggle of conscience about the 'borrowing' and prays for guidance. God means humans to work for their daily bread; that means Hunters too – "by the sweat of your brow." And God, or Jesus anyway, means for us to be our brother's keeper. How can Mama do both? She cannot settle this in her mind. In the day she feeds whoever comes for food; at night she prays God to tell her if she's done the right thing, and forgive her, and show her the way if she hasn't.

One day Teeley came to get sugar and flour, and brought a woodchuck to trade. Mama took it; she said, "Thank you," but she buried it. She said she just couldn't cook that creature and give it to us to eat.

I wonder what thoughts they have of us. We are the newcomers. Hunters have been on the ridge next east ever since the Trail of

Tears. They are Cherokees driven out of their own land in Georgia. They weren't supposed to settle here. They were supposed to walk all the way to the Oklahoma Territories. Most of them died on the way; one of the Hunters' forebears was left here for dead, but he lived. Papa wondered once if it was their family who filled our spring with boulders.

Mama buried that woodchuck. All the same, she didn't feel satisfied. It was food after all. And offered in good faith for food Mama had given their family. The second was the main reason Mama felt uneasy.

I was in the other room, writing a letter to Grandma Rickman. I am now a good letter-writer. Teeley stood in the doorway. Mama met her there. Teeley had on a dress with fancy tucking on the bodice and a row of small buttons down the front. It was a tea dress, not for everyday, and worn, and had not been sewn for her. We know about hand-me-downs because clothes come to us from our cousins. But Teeley's hand-me-down dress was all worn out. It was ready to be torn into rags.

Teeley held a hare by its hind legs. She held it out to Mama. How did I know what it was? Only because the legs were so long. The creature was shiny and bright pink, skinned. It was so strange like that, as if it had lost its name.

Mama reached for it. She said, "Thank you, Mrs. Hunter, will you come in?" Teeley backed up a few steps and ducked her head. She must have said no, and then she went away. Mama watched after her for a little while and then came in. She laid the long, shining body on the kitchen table. She put her hands on the table's edge and leaned into them, bowing her head.

Mama cooked it for us. We ate it.

I think Mama and I had the same thought, that Mrs. Hunter was sorry she had given us an animal that wasn't dressed, and also Mrs. Hunter knew Mama had buried the other one, and she forgave her.

Mama isn't noisy. If you ask me about her everyday voice, she doesn't talk a lot.

Of course, there are prayers. She and Papa pray together in their room, we can hear them, early morning and before bed.

Papa prays at table while we sit waiting and smelling the food.

Mama listens to our prayers at bedtime, after reading and washing and Mama playing the cottage organ from Aunt Mattie. We kneel beside our bed. "Now I Lay Me..." After my birthday, Mama told me I could add on. Oh. There is a lot to say. Mama said, "Be moderate."

Mama's eyes are good speakers. They are blue, they shine, they are calm, they smile and they snap – depending on how she is thinking. Tonight she stands by the stove, looking over our heads at Papa at the door, on the other side of the kitchen. Her eyes are crackling and telling him something all right, and now she is quoting from the Bible. Papa just steps sideways onto the porch.

Mama keeps stirring. Christine scrubs her shoes back and forth on the floor. They never fight, but Mama does that, quotes from the Bible.

*

Teeley is fat, but she is nimble. She almost runs to where we are in the garden, picking green beans. "Miz Emack, do let me help," and she picks up her skirt in front faster than Mama can answer. She knows how, and goes fast down the row, her brown hands quick and careful with the vines.

We have plenty, and we can spare Teeley as much as she needs. She thanks Mama for this, and keeps picking - so much that now her skirt looks like a sack with a pumpkin in it. She keeps picking. Mama notices, but doesn't say anything. Teeley picks more.

All three of us stand, Teeley brushes her glossy black hair from her cheeks with her one free hand, and says Goodbye and Thank you again, Miz Emack. In Dillon's store, on Thursday, Mrs. Dillon sings out to Mama, "So I see Teeley has planted a garden!" What a surprise, and then she says, "She came in to sell me a big sack of beans."

I am dusting. Tiny shiny motes fly up excited, then slow down and float in the band of sun that pours in the window. When I was small, I called the shiny bits sunbeams. When they landed on my arms, I imagined they were fairies. Calling them dust is not magic; I will always call them sunbeams. I am glad I made this decision.

I have to use my whole left arm, up to my shoulder, helped by my other arm too, to dust this heavy book. It is Mama's Doctor Book, the second most important book in our house. I turn the first pages again: made in 1884 by W.D. Condit and Co., in Des Moines, Iowa. Mama didn't study to be a doctor or a nurse; where did she get it? Maybe from her mother.

Mama is the midwife in the Valley. She is also advisor on such matters as stings, burns, fever, broken bones and toothaches. There are pictures of some of these bad-lucks, delicate drawings someone has made with a very small pen. They look gruesome. But Mama is not afraid. She stays calm. When the twins were born, she made lots of noise, but she wasn't afraid.

The most important book is the Holy Bible, and it is not handed-down. Grandpa Rickman gave it to Mama and Papa when they were married. It is also large. I dust it slowly, all over. It has a soft black leather cover, much nicer than the Bible at school that has sharp corners. The letters used to be real gold, but the gold is all worn off, and there are only dents now saying HOLY BIBLE. Every page is rimmed with gold; when the book is shut, its three sides shine like ribbon, with a marker of red silk.

Inside the cover, Grandma Rickman, who can make letters like they did hundreds of years ago, has made tiny paintings around the first letters of the paragraphs about Mama and Papa getting married, Mary Christine getting born and baptized, and George too, and me, and now will she do it for Mark and Elizabeth? The paintings are of trees and waterfalls, delicate deer and birds. These hills and valleys are what the world is like, far away from the Ozarks, and farther away, even, than Wichita. I know that all the world is God's world, but these faraway parts are the best.

*

We know we are poor, because Mama and Papa have to work so hard and because we don't waste a scrap of anything, and because of hand-me-downs. But we were probably rich in Wichita. Our house had a whole upstairs and Mama had a piano. And we are not as poor as most people here. The Hales and Hunters come to us for food, and we have books. We have the Bible, the Doctor Book, the dictionary, and Papa's astronomy books. Papa gets the *American Review of Reviews* by mail every month. No one else in the Valley does; no one else reads the papers every week: the *Kansas City Star* and the *St. Louis Post-Dispatch*.

*

This is a sad story about Teeley.

She came to the door and Mama asked her to come in, and she did. She doesn't come in as often as she is asked. Maybe she and Mama measured out flour and sugar, or went to fetch eggs; then she went home.

That is when Mama noticed her pin with little Willie's hairs was gone. How could it be? She had had it on since morning, but Oh! she remembers now, she took it off when she washed her chemise; she put it right here by the window. But it is not there. It is not anywhere. We get down on our hands and knees, Mama and George and me; it is not anywhere. Next day, Teeley came back with the cup; Mama tells her about the loss, that it was her mother's most loved possession, given Mama in trust for a family treasure.

After a little while, Teeley left.

In about a minute, she came back. "I found it, Miz Emack; I found it on the path."

Mama cups the shining glass bubble in her hand. She has tears in her eyes. She tells Teeley, "I cannot tell you how grateful I am. Thank you."

*

Dr. Steely's son has killed a man.

The twins aren't tall enough to reach the mailbox, so when they see the mailman's buggy down the road, they run through the grass as fast as they can, holding their arms out like wings, and shout Mailman, Mailman! He says Hello, Mark and Hello, Elizabeth with serious politeness, and hands them the mail, which is usually Papa's newspaper and sometimes a letter. Mama has told them so many times it's not proper to open other people's mail, but they can't help it and do it anyway, even though they cannot read. It's usually Elizabeth but today Mark takes the letter, tears off the envelope, and they both run back, waving a piece of paper at Mama, who waves to the mailman who waves back, and she rescues the letter from Mark who is victorious, Here is a letter, Mama!

It is from Aunt Carrie. About Uncle Ed. Aunt Carrie says that we must come get Uncle Ed, that he cannot stay there, that he needs to be in the country. Mama and Papa talk softly at night. Papa will go on the train to get him. It will take all summer for them to come back, maybe half the fall.

Aunt Carrie says it's *crucial*.

*

Papa reads back to Mama the letter she has written to Aunt Annie:

July 26

Dearest Sister,

God brought Christine a baby sister for her birthday on the twentieth, almost in the middle of her party. What a dear sight – four beautiful nine-year-olds, suddenly no longer *little* children, all braided with bows, dressed for Sunday, and their Mamas – Ida Anderson, Rose Martin, Daisy Mirrill and me. We call ourselves The Quartet.

We had just settled when my pains began. I waited as long as I could, Daisy all the while looking at me in the alert way she has, but they began to come close and fast and I had to signal to everyone that the party was over.

Of course, as soon as Ida left with the little girls (Daisy and Rose stayed to help me), my pains ceased, but after dark they started up again in earnest.

In an hour we had little Ruth with us. We wrapped her in one of the white blankets you sent when the twins were born. All that first night she lay in my arms, and the second day, with her eyes fast shut. Through her sleeping face she seemed to be saying, "I am not ready to be here, I am still where I was." My darling connection to heaven! I held her and smelled her sweet skin and whispered to her in my thoughts, "Teach me, baby." Without a sound, without opening her eyes, she agreed she would. I told Mr. Emack about it and he could not but see that yes, this is a special child, special in a wise old way. We have called her Ruth, after Ruth who left her home among the Moabites to go with Naomi to another country.

Word from Kansas City is not good. Carrie writes that Ed has been hallucinating, so George will go by train to get him and bring him to stay with us. It fills me with dread, not only that George will be gone for so long (six weeks!) and me here alone with the little ones, but that life after Ed arrives will be so changed. I know it is

75

charitable and, as George points out, the practical, sensible thing to do. We can use Ed's help here. By the time they get back (they will be driving Ed's horse and wagon), Ed will be dried out, and once he's here there will be no more bourbon.

Where will he sleep? We are just starting to consider *this* practicality!

May God bless you, dear Annie, and keep you always.

Your loving sister,

Mallie

We had Christine's party on Sunday. She is nine. Everybody came! But now we have someone else in our family with Christine's birthday. She is Ruth! July 20.

Mama ended the party. But before she did, Mrs. Martin took out a newspaper from her pocketbook and read from it when all the friends were listening. Some women have chained themselves to the gates of the Governor's mansion in New York. I think it is New York. They object that they cannot vote in elections, that they are being grouped in with criminals and cattle. That makes them non-persons.

The friends are quiet as she reads. Criminals and cattle! More quiet. Then Mama says, "I know my worth." Then everyone talks at once. Mostly that it doesn't seem necessary, since they and their husbands always agree how he will vote. But Pearly's Mama doesn't say anything.

Criminals! Cattle! Of course not; of course they are persons!

Uncle Ed is Papa's older brother; he lives in Kansas City, where Aunt Carrie lives too, but not in the same house. Not much of a life, says Papa. Uncle Ed is also Grandma Mary Belle's favourite child, her firstborn. It is wrong that there is a favourite child. Mama doesn't have one. Neither does Papa. We know we are all God's beloved children; we are equal in his eyes.

But Mama and Papa talk about him while we are falling asleep. Many nights in a row. Where will he sleep?

Papa says it doesn't hurt his feelings, about not being the favourite.

Mama has pinned everything up: her red hair on top of her head, bright in the sun and already springing loose around her ears, and her skirt and apron hiked halfway to her waist so her stockings show. She is ruining her only shoes, she says, but it's no worse than when she's in the garden. We can clean them. Maybe it isn't only the shoes she's fussing about. She has worry-lines between her eyebrows. Or hurry-lines, up and down, three of them. She squints in the sun while she hammers.

Papa has gone to get Uncle Ed. We haven't been told what sort of sickness he has, and it's not like Mama not to say, but whatever it is, Mama thinks he'll be well by the time they get here. Then why is he coming? From the whispers I heard when they were in bed, maybe we will save him from something. Maybe he has lost his faith. In that case, he'll get it back, with all the prayers at our house.

The first thing Mama must do is break boxes apart. These are wooden boxes from Cabool that held freight goods sent by train to Dillon's store; I am helping her, watching out for nails so I won't get a puncture and maybe blood poisoning. I put the nails in a pan and afterwards I'll hammer them straight for Mama to use. We get two boxes every day. Mr. Cooper brings them with the mail from Cabool, and Mama pays him ten cents per box. Then we break them apart into boards and Mama hammers them onto the two-by-fours Papa built before he left.

We are making a room on our house for Uncle Ed. We only need to make three walls, a floor and a roof because the fourth is the wall of our house. Where our window is, we will make a door. Maybe. Mama is thinking about this.

"On the other hand," she says, "he's a grown man and may want his privacy, so maybe we'll just put in a door on the outside."

This is a good idea. The hurry-worry lines smooth out a little bit. Three boards up and down, side-by-side, two short boards crossways at the top and bottom, and a long, slanty board catty-corner, and that's a door.

"I'll nail that thick cardboard from Mrs. Dillon to the two-by-fours inside."

*

Christine is hoeing all by herself in the garden. Usually Papa would be with her, or he'd be out there alone, chop-chopping, and Christine would be with the baby. So a lot is different.

Ruth is the best little baby, sweet as a kitten. No, sweeter. She's the first baby we ever had not to cry when she wakes up. She just opens her eyes and looks around at the air, and after a minute she starts to wave her arms and kick the covers, and then she turns her face to the window where sunshine and the shadow-shapes move. These are exciting; Ruth waves and kicks faster when the shadows quicken.

Then one of us picks her up. Everybody wants to hold Ruth, so she gets carried most of the time.

"But," says Mama, "not near hot water, or if you children are rough-housing." Of course not.

So, though everything is strange, with Papa gone and the house different, and Mama hammering all the day, the strangeness of having Ruth here is good. I, for one, have a lucky feeling.

*

Teeley comes. She stops to watch us. Mama stops hammering and looks at her. Teeley drops her bundle and picks up one end of a board. Mama picks up the other end. They walk around to the back and Teeley holds the board up straight while Mama hammers it to a crosspiece.

I don't know when Teeley told Mama; I didn't notice that they did any talking. But long, long ago in Georgia, before they had to leave, and before they learned log cabins from the French, the Cherokee people lived in round houses made of mud, with roofs made of long grass. The house-builders were the mothers and the wives.

His thing down there was not scary. It was interesting. It was shiny as a doorknob, and long, with a bend. What was scary was the way he held it between his thumb and middle finger and aimed it at us, and the sly, grinnish look on his face as he looked hard at us. He is Hales's cousin.

We ran. Me and Christine, we ran home, full-out, oh, it was only a quarter-mile. We ran and double-took the porch steps and into the kitchen, and I told Mama what happened – everything. Christine told little pieces.

"Mama, he was lying down behind a fallen tree and then he stood up. Mama, he said 'Lookit here, girls.'"

Mama said, "From now on, no cutting across that forty or any of the forties. Take the roads." I think about it almost every day, what it looked like: not a dickey like George's but shivery and alive, like a fat divining rod, like a big asparagus, like the purple hooded bud of skunk cabbage first thing in spring.

*

Papa is home all of a sudden.

He stands, holding the reins to a horse we don't know, and this wagon. A sandy-haired man must be Uncle Ed. Mama cries a small cry and dries her hands and strides out to meet them, and we run. Mama wants only to look at Papa, but she has manners, and looks and looks at him while she looks at Uncle Ed too and says how glad we all are that he is here.

The sandy-haired Uncle Ed looks quiet and nice. His head and his hands shake.

Papa introduces him. "Children, this is my older brother, Edmund. Here from Kansas City to stay."

We grab Papa and hug his legs and around his waist. He cannot walk. Mama's mouth wobbles and she is crying. Papa squats down to hug us truly, and he says our names, and he looks over our heads at Mama. "Oh, Mr. Emack" is what she says.

There are thimbleberries all over the farm wherever there's sun, which is practically everyplace near our house, especially next to the road. That's one good thing. Baby chicks are another, and, not so good, there are blue racers in the grass. We saw one that stretched clear across the road; we couldn't see his head or his tail. Who knows how long he really was? Or she? We didn't stay to find out, Christine and I. We stepped over him quick and ran.

Another summer thing is emptying out last year's mattress fillings, everybody's, and stuffing in new. We do it all in one day, it's such a big job, and we cannot even start until late in the morning when the dew on the ladies' bedstraw has burned off. We wear overalls because bedstraw is scratchy. We wade through the tall plants by the creek, we cut off the tops that look like whirligigs, and fill up the mattresses that Mama made from feed sacks she traded a long time ago. The more you can stuff in, the longer the mattress stays fat, as the leaves get dry and flatten.

Then the best part is going to bed, because the bedstraw smells so sweet. The smell lasts almost all year. Chris and I lie under the eaves and smell and smell and listen to Papa and Mama praying and talking, and we talk too until we fall asleep at the same time.

*

Nobody around us on the farm has an icebox, but last summer and once before that, somebody drove into Cabool and brought back a huge chunk of ice. Everybody in the neighbourhood got notified and then all the mothers or big sisters made ice cream mix. That night all the families went to Merners' or whosoever's house and sat on the edge of the porch turning little freezers, passing them around.

We children did it last year, but not Elizabeth and Mark, of course, but they sat with their legs hanging off the porch like everybody. Mama is very careful. Other families have raw eggs in their custard, but Mama thinks it isn't safe. She knows people get sick sometimes. So ours is cooked, and she makes sure we only eat that.

*

It might be today. In fact, I am almost sure it will be. Last week at suppertime, Mama mentioned that it was getting mighty hot, hot enough for ice cream – almost. Mama is teasing, but I know she's not just making it up. Friday came, though, and Saturday, no ice from town, and then Sunday, and there's no labour on Sunday, and here it is Monday, and hot as firecrackers at only eight in the morning.

Mama has gathered the eggs. There are enough, and she sets the cream to rise, and there's enough of that; she will surprise us later on for sure. She stands in the doorway with my hat while I lace my shoes to the top. It's too hot for shoes, but the fence row is too scratchy for bare feet. My overalls cover my legs. She hands me the bucket. I already know, but "Berries," she says, and shines her eyes at me. Berry ice cream! Mama isn't saying, and I don't ask in words, but maybe for sure it will be ice cream tonight on somebody's porch.

Everybody in the family can pick berries, except Ruth. We divide up the work. Papa, Uncle Ed, Christine and George and me do the field work. Plant. Hoe. Weeds, weeds, weeds. My main job is cutting the suckers from the stumps of trees that don't want to die. I hate getting hot at this work, but I like being one of the big ones. Today, Papa doesn't need me, or has a plan, and tells me to stay behind. He and Christine went early with hoes to the west field, Papa in the railroad cap Uncle Ed brought with him from Kansas City, and Christine in a flat straw hat tied under her chin with a sash from a summer dress. How different they are! Papa tall and fair and sandy-haired and Mary Christine dark as a mink with black eyes that dance. She swaggered off across the yard after him, imitating his long steps, looking back to see if we got the joke.

Mary Christine has told everybody again this summer that she isn't Mary anymore, she wants to be called only Christine. Oh, I wouldn't trade my first name for my middle. If I didn't love Mama so much and did not want to hurt her feelings, I'd tell her I wish she hadn't given it to me: Wildrose. A plant. Mama is doing her best to remember only Christine, but Papa isn't trying, and looks cross when she tells him again, but he doesn't tell her to forget all this name-changing nonsense, as I thought he would.

So it is George and me who will pick the berries. There are such floods of them we have to pick every three days. They are delicious, and good for us, full of vitamins and – what Mama said – proof if we ever needed it that God is good. George's shoes are laced up now, Mama gives him his cap, and we head out.

There is never any doubt about where the ripe ones are; we have only to look and listen. The hedges alongside the road are sprouting blackbirds. They dive in at a hundred miles an hour from all over the mountain, fanning their wings, pushing at one another, making purring, burbling sounds. And bees crowding pale flowers nearby. I feel kindly towards bees, and explain to George that they are a big reason for the berries. He listens with a plain face, but his eyes don't believe me. "Don't get the berries too deep, or they'll squash on the bottom. And don't eat so many; you'll get a stomachache." He doesn't believe this either. Juice streams between his brown fingers and runs under his cuff into his sleeve.

The road beside the patch is dusty, fine and gold and soft to touch. We have had so many sunny days that you can just blow on it and set up a cloud. But the cloud that starts at the skyline and heads our way is slowly becoming Mr. Joliffe's wagon. The Joliffes live west, three crossings up, and I have never visited, but I know Shirley from school, and her family passes us on their way to town. Mr.

Joliffe's Erica draws alongside – her lovely warm brown sides and slender legs – and the wagon, and Mr. Joliffe on the seat. We push through the brambles to say hello. Mr. Joliffe reins Erica in so we can stroke her. He is off to town all right, and he'll be bringing back a fair chunk of ice, figures our mother will want to know that for sure. I holler, "Yes, Sir!" and George, who doesn't understand the meaning of a big chunk of ice, gets excited anyway, and jumps up and down, "Yes, Sir!" I grab his hand. "It's ice cream!" "Ice cream!" hollers George. Mr. Joliffe laughs out loud and clicks his cheek to Erica and twitches the reins. They're off to Cabool.

There are plenty of berries in our buckets. We forget to say goodbye to the blackbirds and bees, and hike fast back to the house. It will be today for sure.

Papa comes in with another peck. He's been to Fisher's orchard, and George with him, and they've picked five – six! bushels of apples. We divide up the jobs: washing, cutting out blisters, black spots, worms – everything you wouldn't want to eat. Mama says, Don't peel, we need the vitamins, and then we slice them coast to coast, poking out the seeds and the seed walls as best we can. We eat the seeds; they are delicious. We must do this work quickly; the sun is shortening each day and we need days to dry the apples. There is a best slice-thickness for drying. When they're done, we'll make necklaces out of them and hang them up. We'll eat them all winter long and be glad – stewed apples, apple sauce, apple pie, maybe a cake if Dillon's has a nutmeg and cinnamon. Nutmeg is the best, a hard little nut that, when you grate smells like how I imagine the South Seas.

It's my job to cart the slices up the ladder to the loft and out the window to spread them on the slanty roof of Uncle Ed's house. Hundreds, one by one a hundred times, each one separate from the others. It takes me a long time. And the sun shines on them and they dry. Until it starts to rain, when it is my job to take them all in through the window so they won't get soaked. It's hard to stay interested, putting them out, but exciting bringing them in because I have to be faster than the rain. When it stops, and the sky clears, I start all over again – slices, slices, out the window, spread, spread, spread. That's when I start jumping off the roof for a reward. I land on my feet and it makes my leg bones holler.

*

Uncle Frank is here, on a holiday from College. Mama says "My baby brother," and reaches up to pat his face. There are two things – no three – to tell about him; he has a very big smile, he is even taller than Papa, who is *tall*, and a sprout of his red hair springs up like a watershoot at the top of his head at the back. He says it is a cowlick. Cowlick!

He says, "Look, here's one in front too." And all we can see is it's a curvy bend for a lot of hairs at his forehead, but none of them shoot up. "This runs in the family," but we don't see it. He says, "Let's go out in the yard and do tricks."

George and I don't have tricks. Christine says, "Neither do I," and stays in the house. Frank first; he stands on one leg and squats, with his other leg straight out in front, and then stands up again. Do it again! Frank says he will in a minute, and George hollers he can do it, but he keels over, and so do I, and now Frank (who says "Not *Uncle*") does it again, and without stopping does it another time! He has been practicing for years.

I do have a trick. I hold onto the ledge above the washing-porch door, pull myself up and put my chin on it, my fingernails all white. Frank says, "Good!" and I do it again. George can too, and then Frank does it. George and I have to practice Frank's trick, and I wobble too much. Mama comes to the door and says, "The competition around this house is vast and constant," but she looks happy, so it's all right. Frank and George and I do the trick. Better than before, but Frank's is the best.

We're done, but "Lookit!" George hollers to Frank, and dashes across the yard straight at him, sure to run right into him, but he doesn't. He rolls a somersault and springs up six inches from Frank's toes. "Good one!" Frank messes George's hair, and George looks up at him in a way that reminds me he misses Papa, away to work in Webb City.

*

Mama says we are all a scalawag. She is pleased and a little bit worried, but not very much.

*

She says George is a scalawag when he learns the swing trick. He learns it to show Papa. Of all of us, he is the only one who can swing that high. The limb is flat-out level with the ground, and thick. It gives a little when George pumps hard, so we know it won't crack, only bend. But still it makes us watch, every second; it won't break, and he won't fall, as long as we do.

*

Papa home! Before dark George wants us all out at the swing tree. Papa says, "That's high enough; I won't push you higher," so George keeps on all by himself. Highest he's ever been! And the ropes buckle, and George is going to fall, but he doesn't, and top of the next backswing he leans and throws himself forward feet first, like a deer who goes over a fence, and he makes it over! but scrapes the seat of his pants. The swing is crazy-swinging all by itself, and George's legs when he lands make a huge wobble. He scoots away from the swing and hops; he punches one hand with the other. I don't know why, but Christine and I are holding our hands over our ears. Papa turns around and comes back, taking in everything.

"Well, George."

George says, "Hoo-eee, Papa."

Christine and I won't try it. Of our whole family, of everybody at school, only George can do it. Go over the limb.

Penna. Ave. & 11th St. PRINCE Washington, D.C.

*

This is Papa when he was a little boy. George says Big ears! Mama thinks he's about George's age, and this is a long thought. Was Papa a scalawag?

Mama says this is Papa before his Papa died of pneumonia. I didn't know that. You can tell by the picture that Papa doesn't know what is going to happen.

Old Whitey is the best hen. She comes up to peck around my feet while I sit on the bottom porch step outside the kitchen. Mama is in there – push push push step step bang step step push push push – doing the ironing. The step step is Mama going from kitchen table to stove and back and the bang is putting the cooled iron down on the hot stove-top again. Then she picks up the other, hot iron and goes back to Papa's shirt. Mama's ironing is beautiful and the backs of all the kitchen chairs wear shirts and dresses pressed brand new. The chairs look like another family, so I make up a story. They will all go to Joplin in the cart. No, two carts, there are too many for only one, and the girls will carry white parasols, all except the Juanita-girl, whose parasol is peach. They will go for a week to a big city, maybe St. Louis; no, too far away. To a rich cousin's house (who?). I cheer at the exciting thought, and Old Whitey (who queenly steps – she walks like the moving of the minute hand on the wall at the train station) makes a fast scramble into the tall grass in the yard.

I call after her, "Whitey, Whitey, you are the best hen!" Old Whitey understands the English language and comes back out. Sometimes I accidentally think that this is the same Old Whitey I had when I was two, and that her first self has come back. I even pretend with her, "Whitey, do you remember the Fisher place and the orchard and the cootts's graveyard?"

Whitey keeps pecking and walks around in a circular way as if she won't hear me. It's because they're both exactly the same, the way they look, and how they both are about chicks. They brood just the same, sitting on their eggs so they won't cool off and die. And when the babies peck their way out, all stringy and wet, and dry off and fluff up and start walking around right away, both Old Whiteys ambulate around the yard – I mean, she did, and this one does – with the little chicks, until they get bigger. And both Old Whiteys fuss and call them in close to her, "coott, coott, coott;" that's how they got their name, the little cootts.

Mama lets the little kids keep a little coott for a pet, maybe there's something wrong with it and maybe not, and then when it dies – it always dies, it's from being picked up all the time – we bury it on the other side of the mossy place, down the slope in the cootts's graveyard.

Early in the summer, Whitey decided against living in the coop with the other chickens. Instead, she has made herself a grass broody-nest in the corner of the privy, just inside the door. She scarcely stirs when we come and go, except for sometimes standing up a bit, ruffling her feathers and sitting down again. She doesn't look at you while you sit there, even if you talk to her or grunt, but she listens. Mama says this is the most outlandish thing to happen around here for a long time.

Her little chicks hatched perfectly and learned to peck, and after a while everybody moved out to the hen yard, but after several weeks Old Whitey came back to the privy. Sometimes we walk down there together.

*

I am dreaming about going someplace. In the dream Christine is home from Joplin and full of stories about high school and her boarding house and the mostly men but one woman who live there. Joplin is big with many streets, many stores, a trolley and a huge library. I ask Christine to repeat about the library: eight or nine wide concrete steps up to double oaken doors, big swinging fans up at the ceiling, long tables with chairs down both sides, and people reading, some of them writing, some of them sleeping, and everywhere, on shelves to the ceiling: books. She has a library card with her name on it, MARY CHRISTINE EMACK, typed by the librarian and signed in ink by Christine. She has her own pocketbook now, she has to, being away from the family in a town, and keeps her card in the pocketbook's black silk slot.

I think I can never learn to wait patiently for high school. I count on going to Joplin with Chris to live with her and wait on table like she does. Mama has never mentioned this, but...

...the afternoon is fat with yellow light and the faint singing of grass flies. Suddenly the sun on the steps where I am turns everything in the world transparent. Time slows down to nothing; small insects flying in so-easy arcs in the tall stems turn to spots of fire. Beyond the road, a bird, too independent to be quiet in the heat of the day, speaks confidentially. I think I never want to leave here. Inside, as if forever and ever, Mama is push-pushing and talking in a peaceful voice to George and Mark. Elizabeth is on the front porch, swinging. I can hear the squeaks of the swing chains. I think I will never, never go.

Old Whitey stitches her way around the dirt at the edges of the rain barrel. Whitey is already old. Whitey would be dead. I hug my knees and rock. But maybe not.

*

I want my legs to fly. Fly fast up the path to the house. All of me to fly like the blackbird, or an angel in the twinkling of an eye. I am holding Old Whitey in both arms. Old Whitey doesn't weigh anything. I whisper, "...don't die, Whitey, you're only sick, don't die, Whitey, only sick." I know that if I can get to the house and Mama fast enough, Mama will save Whitey. I also know Whitey is dead.

Mama comes to the edge of the porch with the dishpan. The soapy water leaps in a long curve from the pan at the end of Mama's arm, but she is looking at me coming through the tall grass. Her face changes as she watches, and she puts the pan down and hurries down the steps. We meet in the grass; we make a case for the little body between us. Old Whitey's head leans sideways too far. Her little red comb makes a tired ruffle on her white feathers, now all air. I hold her. Mama suggests we put her down, take her over to the porch, but I cannot. My thoughts are still saying, Whitey, only sick.

I start to ask God to make Whitey well, but stop. Great waves fall down – dark green and black, and weigh like the ocean sweeping; I cannot stand. Mama holds me up. Three of us stand in the shivering oat grass and a long sound begins. It is coming out of me. I have never heard it. It ends and another one begins; where does it start? Up, and gets huge, and it is too big in my chest, I will burst, and now in my throat and my mouth, it comes out.

Mama holds me, easy and firm, not squashing Whitey, and I cry. I cry and we walk, Mama walks us, to the porch step, and sits us down. Mama rocks me and Old Whitey. I cry and rest and cry more. It will never end. Old Whitey's small round eye is going away.

Restoring The Drowned
Swallowing Foreign Bodies
Clothes On Fire
Boils – Furuncles

Dr. Kellogg's Doctor Book sits like an important person on the sideboard, so secret, but I tell George about Menstruation; he runs away. I call him to come back but he won't. He bends his face into a yuck, and I agree with him, although it is interesting and he won't ever have this happening, and someday I will need my own lots of clean cloths like Mama.

Mama attends to everyone if they are in a hurry or if Dr. Thorne is far away, which he mostly is. He has a problem with the drink, also his wife.

I am proud of Mama; I asked her how she got started. She said it was natural, that everyone should have access to this learning, but Papa mostly doesn't, although the Book is here. Most people don't.

Baldness
Seminal losses (losing seeds?)
Arcus senilis (what is this?)
Boring pain in the bones (this must be wrong)
Mental unchastity (bad thoughts about God?)
I know Baldness, and I know Copulation because of the Hunters, amongst humans.

I would truly like to ask Mama, but she would know I have been studying the Book, and I would be doomed to her sharp look, and too many prayers on my behalf.

*

I cannot go to school. I lost a shoe in the huge mud on the road. The mud sucked it right off my foot. I thought of quicksand, and didn't dare stay in to get it back. My left shoe.

Locust Grove has been our home these twenty years, here on a rise
of land south of Beltsville, Maryland. Mr. Trueman Belt built this
house and lived in it for thirteen years; he named us Locust Grove
after the trees, then left the house empty. We have repaired the house
and outbuildings – the barns, smokehouse, carriage shed, housing
for the pigs, for the chickens, and the ice house. We need every one.
The slaves' houses, of course, down the back lane. Come springtime,
we rise up out of an ocean of daffodils covering the slopes around
us. We cultivate the fields here and across the Turnpike.

I will describe to you my darling Elbert Grandison, a man so very
pleasing to look upon: a blue and steady gaze: his wide mouth
smiles seldom, but when he does – after all this time – he opens my
heart to Heaven. Tall – he is five feet, ten inches, and quite muscular
for no great obvious reason; although he is a farmer (and engineer
for Washington), he tends to a scholarly life.

He has a most wondrous head of hair – Emack hair – brown and
thick in my fingers. I married him for these reasons, and because
my father smiled and said he hoped Elbert would tame me some.

We have six sons living. We lost young Elbert when he was but nine,
and little Charles Calder, only just past a year. I know that Elbert,
too, counts them. We have eight sons.

And we have Eudora Virginia, now seventeen. Our firstborn is James
William named for our two fathers: James, for mine, and William
for Elbert's. He is twenty-three. Ned is our youngest, two years old
(christened Edward). Between these are George Malcolm, Charlie,
Frank and John. And Dora.

As for me, oh, well, perhaps one day one of my children's children or theirs will catch sight of my portrait here on the sideboard. Maybe that reading-child will declare (as I think) that I resemble Miss Emily Dickinson, a Massachusetts spinster, reclusive (as I am not at all) and an odd and compelling versifier, who I hope by then will be better known, so unique a voice, and interesting. Of course, I cannot truly comment aye or nay on that resemblance, but...I can carry on at happy and knowledgeable length about the sideboard – *my* sideboard! Griff and his oldest boy, Jeremiah, spent half the winter making it, after my drawing, of mahogany the Carolina cousins sent north four or five years ago. They had ordered it from abroad for themselves, found they had more than they needed, and thought of us, hurrah! Two drawers side-by-side at the top, bowed up and down, where I keep our spoons and forks, and two cupboards beneath, with doors, and shelves for the china from Mother.

I do go on! It's because it's so new, so beautiful; I know that Griff and Jeremiah are as pleased as I am, and proud of their work. They have rubbed it to a fine gloss – like a rosy mahogany skin.

Now: George, my second born, my daredevil – ever on my mind. When he was young, I taught him to ride: how to saddle his pony, take a proper seat, how to speak with the reins. I did *not* teach him to ride as he has ever since – standing in the stirrups, dashing about the county like a storm. I cannot watch. I tell him You owe a debt of mercy to your animal, but he's off before my words can catch up to his ears.

Elbert may fear for him as well, but I do not think so. He indulges, with pleasure I believe, our son's impulsive nature on horseback, and – now that he is clearly a man – as he joyfully furthers his acquaintance with the young women in the neighbourhood. Only days ago, it seems to me, they were *little* girls, and he and they were entirely careless of one another. Now, when George is about, their Mamas abandon conversation and hover, clucking like disturbed hens. In their nervous presence, I confess it, I feel embarrassed, as if I should apologize for George and his beauty and his intense manliness, altogether. I then feel disloyal, and subsequently dislike them for my discomfort. All the while, Elbert wears his famous benign smile, watching the pageant unfold.

*

There may well be war. A year ago, Mr. Lincoln sent Colonel Lee to Harper's Ferry, to put down Mr. John Brown's slave rebellion. He succeeded, and in less than a month Mr. Brown was hanged, but his atrocious impulse has sparked fire that smoulders here north of Virginia. Brown, who was surely insane, is regarded as a saint in some quarters.

*

We have heard that Lee slept at Blair House that night. Mr. Lincoln had called him from the Texas border, and, earlier in the day, they met. Mr. Lincoln asked him to command the Union forces in what looked to be a certain civil war. For years Lee has been passionate about preserving the union of the states; nevertheless, he declined to accept. The Virginia Assembly would vote on the matter of secession that very night.

Word came in the morning; Virginia would secede, thus joining the seven other states calling themselves the Confederate States of America. Lee, deeply dismayed, deeply a Virginian, rode home to Arlington, thence to Richmond, to assume leadership of the Army of the Confederate States – he, temperamentally the most peaceful of men.

*

James and George would go; they *will* go. The young Turner cousins have already left. James remembers his fealty to his father, and to me too, of course, and comes to us for our approval. George comes as well, but one of his feet is already in the stirrup. There is no question of barring their way. They have already attended that place of first permission – their passion to defend us who depend on slavery to work the farm, and our cousins farther south.

And they have attended that other place, God help us, a conviction that they are impervious to the harms of war.

They will take horses. We will give them money for uniforms. Little Ned is determined to ride up front of James to the end of our lane. Lydia will bring him back. We pack food.

How handsome they are, these sons, these men! Their smiles so broad, faces shining, they wave as if they will be back in the afternoon. It will be months before we hear of them.

The prisons are now under the control of Captain A.C. Godwin, Confederate States Army, as commandant of the post, and are conducted with admirable system and good order. Though properly very strict in the enforcement of the discipline of the prison, Captain Godwin's official intercourse with those beneath his charge is marked with an urbanity and a generous sense of propriety, which appears to have gained him the respect of all the prisoners. He is very efficiently seconded by the following officers, nearly all of whom are young men of marked ability, and of courteous address:

Lieutenant G.M. Emack, of Maryland
Lieutenant F.A. Semple
Lieutenant E.G. Mahler
Lieutenant T.J. Turner
Lieutenant E.W. Ross, of Richmond, Clerk
Captain Warner, Commissary.

FROM RICHMOND: ARRIVAL OF TWO RELEASED UNION
PRISONERS
FROM RICHMOND: MEETING OF THE PROPERTY HOLDERS
OF RICHMOND IN VIEW OF FEDERAL OCCUPATION.

The *Washington Star* of Saturday has the following statement:

Capt. J.A. Farrish, of the 79th New York regiment, and Lieut. J.W. Dempsey, of the 2nd New York, arrived in this city yesterday from Richmond. They were captured at the battle of Bull Run (where both were wounded) and carried to Richmond, and, after a time, successively to Castle Pinckney, Columbia, S.C., and other Confederate prisons, and some time ago returned to Richmond and confined, with about 500 other prisoners, in a building occupied formerly by a man named Libby: a pork-packing establishment.

They left Richmond last Thursday morning in charge of Lieut. Lewis of Gen. Winder's staff, and after being blindfolded, conveyed per a railroad to a station which their guard said was the Summit. Blindfolded, they were put into a car, impressed as an ambulance, their backs to the horses, and started off towards the Federal lines, arriving at General McDowell's headquarters that night. They passed on the way some soldiers, and they thought also some artillery.

They report that on last Saturday night a large meeting was held in Richmond to decide what should be done with the city on the arrival of the Federals. The property holders and most substantial men of the city favoured a surrender, while those who had no interest there were rampant for burning it. Captain Farrish thinks there is a very strong Union feeling in Richmond. Every corner is nightly pasted thick with Union sentiments and mysterious writings, which alarm the secessionists very much.

On last Saturday, and all day Sunday, there was much excitement in the city, and troops were being rapidly sent off while all the artillery that had been sent south of Richmond some time previous was hurriedly brought back and shipped north.

From all that our informants could learn, the Confederates evidently intended attacking Gen. McDowell that night (Thursday) and a large force was hurried off from Richmond for that purpose.

The Confederates at Richmond have every vehicle and cart engaged, busily hauling stones and filling them in the canal and all other boats, for the purpose of sinking them in the James river, on the approach of the Federal fleet.

A man named William Churchill deserted from the 1st Ohio cavalry, and joined the Confederate service. He was placed as one of the guards over the prisoners, and was the most merciless and brutal of all the sentinels – taking every opportunity to offer them insult, and even firing upon them for simply looking out of the window. Capt. Farrish intends reporting this case to the War Office.

They also report that there is a man named Emack, a lieutenant in the Rebel service, who formerly lived in Washington. This man has frequently boasted that he passed through Federal lines at the time of the Bull Run fight, and taking a musket amused himself picking off Federal soldiers. Both Lieut. Dempsey and Capt. Farrish have heard him assert that he has frequent communication with his father, who lives in Washington, and that he knows all that is going on within the Federal lines.

*

(for the *Baltimore Sun*)
The Case of Lt. Emack

Near Beltsville
Prince George's Co, Md., May 15, 1862

My attention having been directed to an article in the *Baltimore Sun* of the 12th inst., copied from the *Washington Star* of Saturday last, in which I have been referred to as holding communication with my son in the Confederate army and implying that he is informed by me of all that is going on in the Federal lines, all of which I unequivocally deny, and I unhesitatingly assert that I have not written a line or sent a message to him since he left home in August last.

In reference to the statement of his having passed through the Federal lines at the time of the Bull Run fight, and amusing himself by picking off Federal soldiers I also feel bound to deny; for on the morning of that day (Sunday, the 21st of July) he left my house to visit relatives in this and the adjoining county of Montgomery and, not over five miles from home, passed the day. This fact can be fully sustained by the most reliable testimony.

It does not become me to contradict the statements of others, and all I can say in regard to the matter is, if my son made the assertions as stated, they must have been in a jocular way, as he has never given me cause to doubt his veracity.

E.G. Emack

*

Libby Prison
June 30, 1862

Dear Mother,

Having the opportunity to again submit a few lines, I will once more gladden the hearts of the inmates of Locust Grove, by a letter.

I wrote a letter and was to have sent it by the last batch of my *poor, oppressed, cruelly treated* and *patriotic family*, but was so intent on sending a lot for my friends, that I entirely lost sight of my own. Perhaps it was all for the best. I read daily the many *handsome compliments* passed on me by those who give me such a *beautiful character* in Yankeedom. I was not aware, until very lately, that I was such a desperate and fiendish character. I have neither bucked or gaged (sic) prisoners, since they have been under my charge, nor had it done, but several have suffered that punishment, and very deservedly. Whenever the Gunboats advanced or Johnston retreated, the Officers of the Day invariably had something of the kind to do. But why need I be writing such stuff? Their praises and curses are alike to me. If the Gent who reigns below is the father of Liars, he certainly has a great many children in Yankeedom.

I was down in Salisbury last week. Uncle James and family are all well, and send their love to you all. The misses Boyle are with Aunt J.M.. Miss Oce has been very ill but is now well. J.W. is in Charlotte. I received a letter from him yesterday. He is well, with the exception of a mashed big toe. Dolly is in town and has been discharged from his company, his time having expired. He is looking well. Ed Mc— is here and well. I have not seen Fred for several months, although he is quite near the City. McLeod Turner came a few days since with 24 prisoners. Tommy and Calder are well and near the city. Billy is up with Jackson, where I expect to be in a very few weeks. Cousin Alice has gone to Columbia, S.C.. I think Pete and the Major are here yet. Cousin A. wrote to Cousin Betty last Sunday week. The Yanks are somewhat chagrined at not being able to take Richmond with their Gunboats. We sunk the Ironclad Gunboat Galene on last Thursday, fight six miles from here, and they don't feel disposed to try us again. At Williamsburg we whipped them badly, and every day we receive dispatches of victorious skirmishes in all parts of the Confederacy. We are confident of victory and the maintenance of our cause.

I wish I could peep in on Locust Grove, now I know it is looking beautiful. I expect to have that pleasure at no very distant day.

I regret to hear of the death of Harry, poor fellow! He was as true a boy as ever lived. Eugene Fairfax was killed at Williamsburg. Mr. Wm. Luce, now a Lt., is in prison here. He was rather surprised at meeting with me.

I received a letter from Cousin Maggie, some weeks since. They were all well except Aunt Dinah who was failing rapidly.

Abe Broyles and Lt. A.E. Jackson, Jr. are both near here. Give my love to all the family, "Mars" Ned particularly. My kind regards to all my friends.

Goodbye.
Your affectionate son
George

*

LOCUST GROVE, SUMMER, 1862

A radiant morning: Margaret has been teaching Lydia to read. Lydia is but twelve, but bright as a copper penny, and catching on fast. The enterprise is a secret between them, except that Elbert knows. He is slightly uneasy, but says little. He trusts his wife's good heart and moderate judgment, and briefly petitions Heaven.

Margaret and her maid are still upstairs. Margaret sits up in bed, the bedclothes strewn with letters from the boys. She has read them many times; she has learned them by heart, but she loves to touch the pages they have touched – so few, and the war going on so long.

Lydia thinks reading will take a long time learning, all the marks so close together.

An abrupt series of blows on a door downstairs; they hear a protesting voice – Oriana – in the kitchen, now heavy bootfalls on the stairs. Lydia is fast. In two swift passes she gathers up the letters, their envelopes, and genuflects to pick up the chamber pot. She crams the letters into the pot and drapes all with a small towel as the bedroom door explodes inward.

Holding her head high – this is not *their* home – Lydia passes the four soldiers now halted at the foot of the bed, and haughtily proceeds downstairs and out of doors. She will hide the letters in the shrubbery behind the privy. When the soldiers are gone, she will bury them where no one will find them. When the war is over, she and Mistress will dig them up. The soldiers are very young. The Lieutenant addresses Margaret. "Ma'am, we are here to arrest Lieutenant Emack."

Margaret cannot withdraw her eyes from the bayonets mounted on their muskets. They stand taller than the young men. "Please leave the bed, Ma'am," and as she quickly does so (and me in my nightdress, she thinks), they set to work, bayonetting her bed. Six times. Eight times.

Did he mean George? Did he mean James? "Lieutenant Emack is not here."

"So you would say, Ma'am."

At last they leave. Every mattress in the house has been stabbed to tatters, curtains have been pulled down, doors and cupboards slammed ajar. Feathers, clothing, books, little shattered treasures – scattered everywhere.

In a cluster, the children come out of the kitchen where Oriana has herded them. Oriana still grips the kitchen poker.

Copyright Photographische Gesellschaft

MASTER, MASTER, WE PERISH!

Jesus arose and rebuked the wind and the sea, and there was a great calm.

—*St. Luke, 8 : 24; Psalm 107 : 23–31.*

"When the storms of life are raging, tempests wild on
    sea and land,
I will seek a place of refuge, in the shadow of God's
    hand.
Tho' He may permit affliction, 'twill but make me
    long for Home,
For in love, and not in anger, all His chastisements
    will come."

POST CARD

THIS SIDE FOR MESSAGE   THIS SIDE FOR ADDRESS

CABOOL
MAY
9
5 PM
1917
MO.

U.S. POSTAGE
1 CENT

Dear Christine,
We have been
dreaming of you
so much lately.
I wish you were
here. Mamma has
been very sick.
Please write right
away. Lovingly
Grandma B.

Miss Christine Bm——
2028 Wall St,
Joplin,
Mo.

NO. 1917 "SELECT EAGLE" U.S. A., BROOKLYN, N.Y.

To: Miss Christine Emack
2028 Wall St.,
Joplin, Mo.

Dear Christine,

We have been dreaming of you very much and wish you were here. Mama has been very sick since Sunday. Please write right away. Lovingly, Juanita E.

I turn over the postcard and the picture is of a wild storm on terrible crashing waves and a broken boat with torn sails. It is dark night, but a bright light shines on the faces of six men who are frightened and hold on tight. Their faces turn to the light and to Jesus:

Master, Master, We Perish!
Jesus arose and rebuked the wind
and the sea, and there was a great calm.
— St. Luke, 8:24, Psalm 107: 23-31

Mama bought this card at Dillon's.

I turn it over again and underline "very" three times. Then I paste on a one-cent stamp.

We're at Aunt Annie's. It's wonderful, like a holiday. Aunt Annie is Mama's big sister, and here at her house we are all, even Mama, Aunt Annie's children, so she says, and she's delighted.

Mama is simply drained. That's the way Aunt Annie said it...*simply drained*, then she saw that I felt afraid, so then she said it was a figure of speech. Of course, Mama is not drained; she's all tired out. That sounds better, but Mama has never been this tired.

Helen, who is Aunt Annie's girl, is my cousin; we are playing in Aunt Annie's room, with the two girls in the mirror. It is impossible for us to go quicker than them, we know they are us. But they are also them. This gives us the willies, good willies. We will fool those girls. We will move so suddenly and so surprisingly that we'll catch them off their guard. Up to now they move at the exact same second that we do (they have to! they are us!), but we are...quick, Helen! The floor bounces, the rainbow from the edge of the mirror bounces all over the wall.

So tired. She knows we are here playing with the mirror. Before, she would be telling us to shush. Now, all day she sits in the next room on a still chair with our baby in her lap. She isn't really holding Ruth; she is being a lap for her, being a cradle. Ruth is sleeping, so small. When she wakes up she waves her arms and looks at Mama. Mama nurses her and she sleeps some more. Mama doesn't even sigh. She doesn't look outward at us. But she doesn't look inward either. Her eyes are on a ledge in between.

Aunt Annie says it's not unheard of and it's certainly not a sin. You are to believe me, and do not try to hurry back to your usual self; it's impossible.

Mama sewed her blue dress. Aunt Annie will call her when it's time for dinner. Mama is like the Sphinx, holding the desert down.

Aunt Annie asks me what I like about going down to our creek at home. I tell her it's the flying things – the dragonflies and the small green shiner-flies – and the little minnies shooting this way and that in the shallow water. Step-stones. And the water striders with tiny bubbles of air under each foot, how they don't-go and don't-go and then go quick, how they eat very small things that I can't even see.

I also like the woodlot, and then to go through the fence into the free range. Aunt Annie asks me "Why?" and I say "Cows and birds and kissing." "Kissing?" and I am surprised too, that I said that, and "Yes, the Hales and the Hunters kiss in the high grass out there." I tell her that I don't like looking at them kissing because their mouths get all mixed up.

Aunt Annie laughs. I look at her quick to see if it's me, but it isn't, she's just surprised, so I tell her more, about how they roll around and groan, with their buttons undone, and keep on kissing. All the time they're moving so much, their mouths are all mixed up. Aunt Annie has a funny thought-smile on her face, and she asks me if I told Mama, and I say, "No, I forgot."

I say, "It isn't all the Hales and Hunters, only two, and they're mating, like creatures do, except that creatures don't kiss."

*

Today I feel embarrassed, and I can't seem to say anything to Aunt Annie about the kisses on the mirror.

I was experimenting. It was interesting to get so face-to-face close to somebody else (me). I looked all blurry and couldn't see myself except for the huge side of my nose. Unless I closed that eye and saw the *other* huge side of my nose. Then I stood back and looked at myself in the eyes, and there I was, looking right back, and I didn't like it, that I looked stern like that, for kissing. So I said, "Oh, I love you," and got closer. This was not good either, because even though in the mirror I was saying "I love you," I was still watching with eagle-eyes. So then I closed my eyes.

I closed my eyes and said in a love-voice, "Oh, I love you, I truly do," and moved in close. It was a bit worrisome, that I might bump my head on the glass and ruin the experiment, but I didn't. My mouth reached the mirror first. It was cold. I wanted to practice anyway, so I did, six or seven times, and tried it with my mouth a little bit open, my mouth closed, and my mouth pretty wide open, and I practiced thinking *love* while I kissed. It was nothing much, and my tongue got in the way.

I didn't know I'd left the kisses on the glass until I saw Aunt Annie rubbing them off.

We couldn't all stay with Aunt Annie. There were too many of us, especially after the rain began. It rained straight for eleven days. Helen and I were too sad that I had to go, and I asked Mama if I couldn't please, please stay with Helen. Or she come with me. Mama just looked like she couldn't do or say anything, and looked at Aunt Annie, and Aunt Annie was sharp with me that I mustn't press Mama, so George and I went to Uncle Owen's. Mary Christine and the twins went to Aunt Mattie's. Mama and Ruth stayed.

So, that was the whole summer.

Now our family is together again, but we are not at home. We are in Webb City. Our house is white, and is on a corner, and that is good, because we have three yards: one on the side, one in front and one out back. Mama lived in Webb City when she was a little girl, and friends come to see her, people I do not know, who hold both my hands and say "…just so glad to know you at last."

Papa has a job.

"It's sheer necessity. Papa has to earn money and I have to get completely strong."

Papa works at the zinc and lead mine. Breathing there is bad for his lungs, but he says we need the money so we can go home. That is good, the money, and we are all together.

Ruth is bigger than she was at Aunt Annie's, and Mama's red hair is turning white. I hate that these two things happened while I was gone. I am taller too, which I can see comparing to George, and he calls me Stringbean, but it's because he doesn't like to be short.

I have a bigger bed. Mama doesn't know where she'll put me when we go home, I've grown so.

Uncle Ed is taking care of the farm, the creatures and the garden. Papa says Uncle Ed is building himself a small house at a distance from ours.

Tomorrow the photographer comes.

*

Mama says Come home quick from school and change, change into our white clothes. It's a tradition. She has ironed our best things and hung them on the chairs in the kitchen. The kitchen smells like starch and hotness. The ruffle on Christine's dress stands straight up, George's shirt is stiff as a board. Mama cut off the old buttons and sewed on beautiful new ones, made of the insides of shells, all in a line on the top of George's shoulder.

Christine saw him today on Delaware Street, the goat and the cart he pulls. He isn't clean; he's a dirty white and has a beard. The cart is black, painted with a wavy golden line and a golden curlicue on each side. There are two seats, a high one in the back, and a low one in the front.

That's where we will sit and pretend we are going somewhere; the man will hide his head under a black cloth and take our picture.

*

He did. He came after school and hitched the goat next to our house and sat Mark and Elizabeth and George in the cart. Christine stood beside, holding Ruth. Christine's hair bow stood up perfectly like Mama told it to, and we all wore white except that Ruth's bonnet is pink. And me. The thing about me was, I'll tell you later, I got home too late to change and so there I was, all navy-blue. The photographer didn't mind, but Mama did. She bit her lip.

The photographer told me to move in closer...closer to Christine holding Ruth, and look over here, and he ducked his head under the cloth and he waved some feathers up in the air, which was a surprise, and there was a big opening and closing sound, and that was the picture taken.

Mama paid him half the money. She'll give him the rest when he brings the picture. It's exciting to watch Mama open her pocket and take out her green purse and unclasp it. She took out one dollar!

If Papa wasn't at the mine, we wouldn't have this money. And we wouldn't have penny-dolls. We each have four, me and Elizabeth and Christine. They are straight up-and-down dolls, only as tall as my big finger. They can't move their legs or heads, but their arms move by a string through their body. Every doll wears a different costume!

*

Almost every father in Webb City works in the mine. Papa has to go early, so he wakes us children up at the first crack of dawn so we can have prayers and breakfast before he goes, and then he looks at Mama over our heads and their eyes shine at each other, and he takes dinner in a pail and goes out the door. Mama says, "Goodbye, Mr. Emack."

Prayers are too long. I close my eyes and think about going back to sleep or think about Esther or breakfast. Sometimes Papa reads a passage from the Bible, and reads and reads until Mama clears her throat. The passage is about something Papa wants to teach us, but I don't know what it is. The New Testament is easy, but the Jeremiahs are hard. Mama says it's a good thing Jesus came along; otherwise we'd still be hurling rocks at harlots.

There is a cement sidewalk across the street, but on our side it's dirt, hard as a rock, with bulgy roots heaved up that can trip you. Christine and I cross the street to go to school, so that we can skip rope on the way. We go that way again before suppertime when we meet Papa.

We see him coming a long way off. Papa's legs are the longest of anybody's, and he swings his arm with the pail. Maybe he has his coat over one shoulder, holding on with his other hand. If it's not cold out. We see the other fathers too, but mostly we see Papa. Then the little kids start to run, Mark and Elizabeth, and we do too, but we let them go first.

And Papa crouches down and puts his coat and pail on the ground, and the twins run at him a hundred miles an hour, and they bump into him so hard, and Papa hollers Ho and scoops them up all at the same time, and he jiggles them up and down and carries them for a block. Not a whole block, because he has to pick up me and Christine and George, one at a time because we're big, and Papa says,

"How much longer do you suppose I'll be able to do this?" And we laugh because we know it will be a long, long time.

Then Papa started picking up Alice. Alice's Papa walks with Papa coming home, but he doesn't pick her up. Then Alice, she started before Hallowe'en, started running right after the twins. She hops up and down and waits for her turn. She run-walks beside Papa while he's got the twins, and he looks over at her father doing nothing, and when he puts the twins down, he picks up Alice and jiggles her for three houses. She grabs his face so he'll look at her. George and Christine and I wait. By this time we're almost home, Papa gives us a little turn each, and now Papa's face is pink and all smoothed out.

Esther's hair is exactly like the angels' hair in the books; it's curly like a round hat around her head, and silvery-gold. She has blue eyes; I would especially love to have blue eyes. She is so beautiful I peek at her all the time. There is a smile on her face even when her mouth isn't smiling.

After school, we walk home. Right to my face, she talks admiring things about me. She loves my *brown* hair! She says she wishes hers would grow long like mine, but it can't. She asks if I braid my own hair down the back or if I have to get Mama to. She says her mother sews all the clothes in their family. I say So does my mother. I tell her how I wish my hair didn't get caught in the buttons on the back of my dress. I stand in front while she looks, and she tries to think of a way for it not to, but she can't.

"Would you ever cut your hair?"

I look at her short curls. Mama would not let me cut my hair.

I intend not to tell Mama about the nice things Esther tells me; she might think I am tempted to be proud, which is a deadly sin. I don't think it is, if I don't show off.

Esther invites me to her house so she can show me to her mother; I tell her that Mama would *love* to know her. She says, "Can I come play at your house?"

"Yes," but then I'm not sure. We have chores. And prayers.

I walk as far as Esther's corner. I'm worried about getting home late. I am supposed to come straight home. So far I haven't told Mama that I'm walking this long way from school, but I told her about Esther, how she is like an angel, and how she is my best friend and I am hers.

That is why I was home late on the picture-taking day. I had to walk home with Esther first, and she lives four blocks on the other side of school, and we don't step on the cracks. I couldn't help it. You should see her. She is beautiful and nice and already has many second teeth.

Uncle John comes today with milk and butter. He has come three times already. It's hard work; he walks down our street with the milk can in both arms and it is heavy.

He doesn't really have to walk; he could drive; he has a two-seater surrey, shiny and decorated all around its roof with swishy black fringes, like a party. Not a usual carriage for a farmer, says Mama, but isn't it nice? He leaves it on the other side of Division Street because we live on the negro side. Grandma Amanda is in the carriage; she lives with Uncle John in the country, near Noel, where Grandpa William Marcus was a Methodist preacher long ago until he died.

When he comes, Mama asks Uncle John for all the news, and is their Mama any better? How fortunate that John takes such good care of her! Mama cries because she misses Grandma, and because Grandma thinks she is at home on the farm. She would be very upset to know where we live now, in this house.

Last time, I asked Uncle John if I could walk back with him so I could see her. I have never seen her since I was very small, and I cannot remember her face. He said, Yes, I could come, but I wasn't to mention who I am.

She was bundled up and sleeping; I could only see her ear and some of her hair sticking out from her bonnet. I am pretending to write Grandma a letter:

Dear Grandma Amanda Owen, Mama says I would like you but you look as old as witches. Maybe there's an itchy bump on the side of your nose where a hair springs out. Maybe I would like your other side, so I would amble over, but you'd turn and another hair would spring out.

Mama showed me the little square brooch you gave her, with the reddish hairs like thistledown inside, under its bubble of glass. It's hardly as big as two tears. They are baby Willie's hairs, Willie born in the winter and carried off in seven weeks by something hot and tough that won against the prayers.

Maybe you laid your head down on the table at suppertime like Mama did one time, all worn out, too tired to cry (we kids sat still, it was good she pushed her plate away, she would have beet juice on her forehead, and it was queer to look down at the top of her head, at the comb-stripes, and the rims of her ears).

Maybe baby Willie came to you in the shape of a dream of a bird with blue feathers. Here I am in Heaven, he said, and he blew on the bump and the hair, and they all three flew and soon he sent down Mattie, round little sister who probably will live ninety-eight years and die in her sleep by mistake before her breakfast, and by then you'll be in Heaven with Willie, and be glad.

Your granddaughter, Juanita

I might believe in reincarnation. I'd be glad if I did because it's too much of a waste to live and live and go to school and then just die. But the bad thing is, Esther says that you don't get to pick how you come back. You might come back as Roxy's colt, for example – a horse! Well, that isn't so bad, but what if you came back as a bug or a sorghum plant? What if I died and came back into my same family? Well, maybe not this very one, but a cousin? Then I'd come to our house as soon as I could talk and say, *Mama, Papa, it's me, here I am.*

It couldn't work, because Mama and Papa would be dead already. But if they weren't, they'd be joyful. Papa would sit me down and ask questions about where I'd been, and I'd say, no keeping it a secret like it is now. I'd describe heaven, all about it.

Which makes me think about hell. I'm sure I wouldn't go there. I am not sure, but if I'm good from now on, I won't.

Maybe, if reincarnation is true, hell is nowhere. Esther says Buddhists don't have hell. What a good idea. I will ask Mama what about Buddhists. They must be different from Methodists – no Jesus.

But I don't want her to say there's no such thing as reincarnation. It's a very good idea, except for the part about maybe coming back as an onion or something else that might get eaten.

Esther told me something new, that probably we were here before. That I am probably not myself or who I was before. I hate this thought. There is nobody I could have been, even someone wonderful like Rose Red or Joan of Arc, instead of myself.

Here is another thought. All the George Malcolms in Papa's family

– are they the same one born again and again? No, because there's Papa and George, both here now. But maybe George is George Malcolm two back. But then, who was Papa? A same person with another name? Elbert Grandison, for example? Oh.

I told Christine about reincarnation, that maybe we never die. She knows about it already. She says, what good is it if you don't know you're you? I agree with that. But maybe people aren't trying. While I am dying, I will think hard about myself and say, *Me, Juanita Wildrose, me, Juanita Wildrose*...Christine says it's no use, we forget, no matter what. I ask her how does she know? She says because nobody's told us about remembering, and as far as I know, that is so. Maybe Esther knows somebody who did it.

I intend not to die. Then this won't happen, forgetting myself. So far, everyone has died. But probably I will not.

Before bed, all of us children hung up a stocking, and, this morning – treats. This Christmas isn't as exciting as last year's, when Papa found oranges and we each got a round mysterious shape in the toe, which was an orange. George ate his before breakfast, but I saved mine until Mama told me to eat it before it turned into marmalade. Marmalade.

Sugar sticks for all of us, and handmade books from Mama, who drew the pictures too. We sing *Stille Nacht, Heilige Nacht* in English, and *Hark The Herald Angels*. Elizabeth got a little doll from Japan (am I too big for a doll?) and Uncle Ed, who is here, went outside and smoked new tobacco.

We always eat chicken for Christmas. Also mashed potatoes and carrot pudding with brown sugar sauce (last year, orange sauce). I help make the sauce. Papa kills the chicken by wringing its neck. It takes Mama half the morning out back, pulling out the feathers, singeing the skin, yanking out the chicken guts.

"Careful!" Mama says to nobody, pulling out the liver. Attached is the bile sac – the greenest little thing I ever saw. "And," Mama says, "the bitterest little thing you ever tasted if it breaks."

*

Mama is chopping off the chicken's feet to boil for chicken jelly. Before she gets them in the pot, George grabs one in each hand and starts horsing around. He makes a toothy face and runs towards me, waggling the claws. I know he's George, but he seems like a giant scary chicken. Mama says it's important that I not let my imagination run away with me. This is a good idea, but I don't know how.

This is true of many good ideas: to be good, for example. It is a mysterious good idea, and hard to do.

We look at the feet in the pot and I think they are surprised. "Where are we now?" See! That may be so, and if it is, *they know who they are*, even if they are so-called dead.

I'm hanging upside-down over the arm of the green chair, watching Mama's legs and shoes walk back and forth on the ceiling, which it is now, queerly striped brown and another brown. Watch out! Your eyes will stick, Mama says, and never go back, and I believe her because she's truthful, but I'm testing it out because she might be wrong about *my* eyes, so I keep staring at the tip of my nose to do the trick. I have tried in the kitchen mirror to see what I look like staring so, but my eyes plus the mirror double and triple me and overlap so much that I can only get a tiny glimpse of what I look like in all those slices.

I don't talk about this, and also I do not mention the swing, me pumping hard and holding on tight, bending, bending back, my hair swishing the grass, the trunks of the two white oaks whizzing past, how I lean into the other world that has no fences, the world where everything, everything streams into Somewhere, Real.

On good weather days, the doors of the church kitty-corner from us stand wide open, and we, clear across the road, can hear them in there, clapping and singing. Mama rolls her eyes a little to Papa, not noticing we children can see, and I know she thinks it isn't seemly; Methodists are quiet.

But she likes the Robinsons. Mr. Robinson is the preacher, and their family lives next door to us. They like me and I like them, and I like going to their house, and they asked me if I want to go to Sunday School. Yes!

I ask Mama and she says it's all right, she supposes; it's only just across the street. Afterwards, she quizzes me. I tell her all about it. How we go into the back of the church through a wooden blue door with no window, then down the steps into the basement. It is like being inside of a radio; the ceiling above us shakes and thumps, people are stomping their feet and clapping hands. And they sing! Mama says some of the older ones were slaves, and their mothers and fathers born into slavery. They are glad, glad, to be free.

"Perhaps it was the singing kept them going all this time."

After, and in between all the hymns and the clapping and stomping, the prayers. Louder than Papa, and not as respectful. Mr. Robinson talks to God practically man-to-man. I've seen him. He never even bows his head; he stands up straight and talks up to the rafters and beyond to Heaven, and says, "Thank you, Lord!" and doesn't say Thee and Thou.

Everyone butts in. They holler, one by one, and in bunches all together, AMEN! YES LORD! GRANT US! and aren't ashamed. I've been telling Mama about this.

"There are people over in the corner, whose job it is to keep the praying going, and Mr. Robinson going, and they are called the Amen Corner."

Wonderful! is what I think, and wonder how Mama knows that, and I'll ask her after, but now I tell her I wish I could be upstairs too.

Papa says I can look on Sunday School as good work, God's work, that "every penny, Juanita, you give to God, every song you sing, every prayer for your betterment and the betterment of the forsaken, that is you doing God's work."

What I like best is the stories. Mrs. Ebert and her sister tell us about how Jesus raised Lazarus from the dead, how he loved him so much, and his sisters too, that he said, "Lazarus, wake up and pick up your bed and carry it away," and Lazarus felt Jesus touch him, and he did it. *That* is God's work! After high school, and after college, I may learn how to do it, if by then we'll know how. Will I turn water into wine? Mama and Papa say that wine is not in God's plan for our family, but Jesus made it for his friends.

Some miracles can be explained some other way: the loaves and the fishes for example. I think that all those people were hiding their food, but they changed their minds when they felt Jesus' goodness, and then shared.

Mama quizzes me. I can tell by the way she holds her head and the quick look in her blue eyes that she wants to make sure it's all right for me to be going to the Robinsons' church. It's because Mama was raised Methodist and Papa was brought up Episcopalian. "And does anyone suggest that you be baptized, Juanita?"

And I say, "No, but Mr. Robinson asked me if I was baptized, and I said I already was, and he said, "That's *good*.""

*

After this, Mr. Robinson tells Papa that our whole family is welcome to come on Sunday. Ruth wants to go. She has a song. So on Sunday, Ruth, who is only two, sings "My Kitty" at the front, standing on a box so we can see her above the railing. Mama holds her hand so she won't fall. Ruth looks at Mama the whole time, the verse and the refrain. She is not shy at all. This is not a miracle, but it is a surprise.

My kitty has gone from her basket,
My kitty has gone up a tree,
Oh, who will go up in the branches
And bring back my kitty to me?
Bring back, bring back,
Oh, bring back my kitty
To me, to me

all the way to the end, to the tune of *My Bonny Lies Over The Ocean*.

We are home from Webb City, and Mama got baptized today. The Russelites did it. Mrs. Wicks asked them to, and Mama told them that was what she wanted. It's because Mama didn't feel saved. We went with her, all of us – Papa, Christine, George, the twins, and Ruth and me. All of us dressed up, including Mama, whose best dress got soaked. After, Papa put his coat on her so she wouldn't show through her clothes.

Mrs. Wicks said, "This is a joyful day!" But none of us feels that way, not even Mama, whose eyes don't sparkle the way they used to. Maybe the joy will come back slowly, now she's been baptized. Maybe it doesn't happen all at once like a miracle.

There aren't very many Russelites around here; they came from South Texas, and they take turns being the minister, so it was Mr. Wicks who dunked Mama under. It was at the little creek that runs into Elk Creek. Papa said it was a nice little pool, with willow trees bending over to touch the water, and an easy walk in. Mama waded in with her shoes off, and Mr. Wicks came to meet her; he took her hand and led her out deeper. Then he raised his head up to Heaven while Mama looked down at the water, and he began the baptizing:

"The Holy Gospel of Our Lord Jesus Christ GLORY TO YOU, LORD JESUS." (I got the words from Mama.)

"John the Baptist preached, saying, 'The one who is more powerful than I is coming after me; I am not worthy to stoop down and untie the thong of His sandals. I have baptized you with water; but he will baptize you with the Holy Spirit.' In those days Jesus came from Nazareth of Galilee and was baptized by John in the Jordan River. And just as He was coming up out of the water, He saw the heavens torn apart and the Spirit descending like a dove on Him. And a voice came from Heaven, 'You are my Son, the Beloved; I am well pleased with you.' The Gospel of the Lord. PRAISE TO YOU, LORD JESUS."

The sun shone on Mama. While Mr. Wicks held her hands to her chest, she held her breath and bent her knees and leaned backwards, and Mr. Wicks made sure her head and whole self got under, and he said, "In the name of the Father and of the Son and of the Holy Spirit, I baptize thee, Maria Malvina."

Mama came up streaming and her red hair almost black. Mr. Wicks still had hold of her hand, and he lifted up their two hands and his face and spoke directly to God to be the main person on Mama's behalf:

"Father in Heaven, who at the baptism of Jesus in the River Jordan proclaimed Him your beloved Son and anointed Him with the Holy Spirit, grant that Maria Malvina baptized into His Name may keep the covenant she has made today, may she boldly confess Him as her Lord and her Saviour, who with You and the Holy Spirit lives and reigns, one tremendous God, in glory everlasting. Amen."

Everyone on the bank said loudly, "Amen!" So did Papa and so did all of us. Of course God was well pleased with Mama, why wouldn't He be? He has known her all her life.

This was Mama's second time of getting baptized. Her father did it the first time, when she was a little girl and a Methodist in Webb City.

*

We hear Mama weeping and telling Papa in the night, "Oh, it was a petition! This time I knew what it was meant to be and I knew what I wanted. It was to be apocalyptic, everything changed: a white moment, bending back, looking at the blue sky and the high feather-clouds and saying *Goodbye, sky, I'll see you in a minute and*

I will be changed...everything different after this. And then water came over my face, cool and into my ears and I felt myself resist, then I thought fiercely, *Thy will be done...Thy will be done...*to let the river and the pressure of Andrew's hand flat on my forehead to have their way, and me be willing to say Yes! even to dying to all I was until now...But I stiffened; my spine said *No,* and I didn't want to be saying it. *No,* even knowing that No was to Jesus, Who died for me, Whose requirement was that God be first. And my heart is broken and I said to God, *I can't.*"

Mama blows her nose. "Mr. Wicks – Mr. Andrew Wicks – looked at me with glad expectation in his eyes, and I could not hide, but I could tell he did not see, that it hadn't happened, not this day, not for him or for Him, not for Maria Malvina, me, my parents' daughter, on this day. You met me, all dripping wet, you put your coat on over my dress and held my hand, and we walked away, the children after us, up to the road. I felt a faint, true gratefulness that you didn't expect me to...anything. Tonight, after supper, didn't the children chatter endlessly? Didn't the sun stay up for hours?"

It was true. Papa put his coat on over her dress, all stuck to her skin. He took her hand and they walked up the path to the road. We children followed after.

After supper, Christine and George and I played hide-and-go-seek for a long time, the twins running around after us big ones, hiding, or seeking, they didn't care. The sun stayed up for hours.

A few days later, Mama wanted to teach me, to tell me about John the Baptist, that he had to have been a large and muscular man. He must have had such power in his hands and arms that he'd hold you under whether you would or no, and you'd start to drown; you'd start to give up, and give up, and you'd say, It's over, my life is over; thank you, sweet life. Thank you Mama, Papa, goodbye Christine, George, Mark, Elizabeth, Ruth...and then your lungs would start to burst, and just as you were at the edge between thankfulness and bursting, he'd let you go – up – into air and light and Oh! you'd be so glad to breathe to feel your wild, starving lungs grab the air, you would feel it – Thank you, Lord, for my life.

*

When summer was half over, Mr. Wicks came on his tall horse who is Samuel and wonderful and smart. We stroked his beautiful nose like velvet and Mama took Mr. Wicks to the porch, but they didn't sit down. He said, "Malvina, you walk slowly this summer." Mama said, "I have been low. I had hoped that the baptism would free me." Mr. Wicks said he had hoped for her too. He had prayed that day that he would help her, help each one of us that day, to pick up a sword, to lose neutrality.

Mama said she was amazed, and told him she was anything but neutral. She was desperate and begging for the Holy Spirit to enter her. Mr. Wicks kept on, not finished, and said he had wanted Mama to have a madness for Him, a complete madness to do His work. Mama said, "I can see, Andrew Wicks, how you became a preacher."

After he left, Mama looked lonely. Papa came in early from the barn and said they would take a walk. Mama took his arm and said, "I imagine I mystify you, Mr. Emack."

She stopped at the roses still blooming on the side of the house. "Do you think my education ruined me for Christ?"

Mama sits more still than we've known her. Her whole self is full of breath she's holding onto. She cannot believe it. It isn't just what it is, her present; it is that Papa has brought it into the house without her knowing. And he has made such a splurge of spending. It is a surprise; from her face, maybe a miracle.

Elizabeth is sounding out its title: "Odeesee."

"Odyssey," says Mama, in a whisper. Elizabeth looks doubtful but Mama is hushed and holy.

"Mr. Emack..."

Papa has two looks. One is watching Mama's face and the other one is shy.

Mama holds it in prayer hands. It has a soft grey cover and the letters are in white, dented in – THE ODYSSEY.

"Is it stories?" asks Mark.

"Oh, son, such stories..."

Now she and Papa are excited, talking back and forth. They know the stories already!

"It is a funny name," says Elizabeth, "the most funny."

This is the second very big thing to happen. The first is the cottage organ. Aunt Annie doesn't want it anymore (she bought a piano), and she sent it to Mama on the train on Thursday. We went in the wagon to get it at the station. These four days, Mama plays it while we are washing for bed. It is big in our house, but interesting – all its keys and pedals and Mama loves it. She pumps with her feet, and she plays the keys with her fingers and she stares at the music book with her eyes. Pump pump – it is hard work all over.

Mama's best birthday in her life.

NIGGER

Mama says Papa has a Nigger Mammy.

What is it?

Grandma Mary Belle hadn't enough milk in her breasts when Papa was born, so she gave Papa to her servant to nurse, who had a little boy of her own, the same age.

She was his *real* Mammy?

Yes, and Papa calls him his Nigger Brother.

I never knew about them. I never heard Papa say Nigger.

Only when he refers to them. They call themselves that; she calls herself Papa's Nigger Mammy. It's a habit. When Papa says My Nigger Brother, he feels love and it means My Other Brother.

We say Negro.

Yes. They are still in Kentucky, at Versailles. Where Grandma Mary Belle was raised and Papa was born. Grandma's father was a Mr. Wooldridge and her mother was born a Moss. They lived next to each other, their two plantations. Her father went to Harvard.

Does Papa still know them? What are their real names? – Nigger Mammy, Nigger Brother?

*

Mama is skimming cream. One of us will ride it into Dillon's.

"I want you to know about Papa when he was a boy, and his thoughts about Negroes. Juanita, I thought you were shocked about Nigger

Mammy and Nigger Brother."

Oh...

"No, I'll just answer your questions, all of you. First, though, I'll get Papa's graduation essay. He went to a fine school in Kentucky; his teachers were conscious of their time, and aware that white people have a responsibility, I'll go..."

She finishes the last of the cream into jars and goes into their room to the bottom drawer that keeps papers and some other significant things. We sit still at the table and wait. Mama comes out and sits down.

Seven pages. At the top of the first: RACE EDUCATION.

Mama reads: RACE EDUCATION, Graduation Essay of Geo. M. Emack, 1894. There's much I don't understand, but when she gets to the part about education, I listen very carefully.

> The advocate for the common and higher education of the Negro race has three propositions to make to the question, "Why educate them?"

> 1st, because they have an intellect which can be made useful, and which would otherwise be thrown away; 2nd, because they help to form the freest and proudest nation on the globe, and 3rd, to stop the great flow of immorality and secure justice in elections for the stability of good government.

> That the negro has a mind capable of development is abundantly verified by the negro of America.

> Although the race has existed in this country as bonded slaves for centuries, yet there never lived in the history of man, a people who have in so short a period so successfully risen from their barbaric state to their present condition as a civilized nation, as this people...

Ours is a country which is honoured by all the world; we have a plan of instruction which far surpasses any other; the grandest constitution that has ever united so many people under one banner of Liberty and we have an inspiration which causes us to believe that our nation will in future far excel any (all) others.

But there is one dark stain on the fair fame of this land of freedom. It is the uneducated coloured population...

Is there not enough around us to open our eyes? Does not plain reason tell us something must be done? Aye! and that too without a longer delay.

Then look! ye lovers of Freedom, throw off the veil of darkness, open your eyes to the condition of things, join your hearts and hands in this grand work of Deliverance, and fleeting time will soon hasten the day when we with one accord can repeat with honest pride, "What the Union thinks today the world will think tomorrow"!

Sometimes I see people from afar off and I know about them. That man on the sidewalk – how he doesn't even step around the wads of tobacco the men have spit. How he just steps and steps and doesn't think about yesterday or even this morning. His head comes out of his shoulders as if he has no neck at all, and even when he is taller than somebody he seems to be looking up at them. He has no hat. His hands make little movements up and in front as if he starts to ask and then changes his mind. Mama says he is a drinker; he is so lonesome is what I think, but Mama hurries us past him. He will be gone from town soon. "There is nothing here for him" is what Mama says.

*

Papa is wise and smart about the Negro race. I will ask him what about this man.

Old Nellie is old and Papa says we can't ride her anymore. Then he says, *This is her time to rest before she dies.* We children don't think of anything to say; we never thought of her dying, just being old.

Roxie. She's a whole other kind of horse and doesn't take kindly to the saddle. Heavens, she doesn't take to us bareback, never mind saddle. But I will ride her, I will, yes. Maybe Old Nellie – ho ho – could give her friendly lessons. Thinking this way, not riding Old Nellie, not wanting Roxie (really Roxanne), I have the idea to saddle up the calf.

The calf is almost grown, not just little. I've never *seen* anybody ride a cow, but I saw a picture once – in a book? – somebody named Lily or Molly or another milkmaid name, riding a cow. Well, I had nothing to do and I just went to the barn and got Mama's saddle and carried it over to the pasture. The little cow looked pretty. She doesn't have a name; we don't name the cattle. I put the saddle on her. She shifted her feet, that's all. So I cinched it under her belly. That's where I made a mistake, not tight enough, or maybe she blew up when she felt the saddle. Anyway, I put my foot in the stirrup and got on top, and then everything got fast. First thing, she jerked back and forward and sideways all at the same time, and I held on and then she started to run, and jumped and rocked – well, she was bucking! It was fun, I loved it.

Then the cinch slipped. I felt it start, but this calf was jumping so I couldn't do anything. At first I thought, good, I'll hold on and pull over to the left and get it back where it was, the saddle, but quicker than I could think it, it slipped more, and then a lot, and then my main job was to get my feet out of the stirrups and fall off.

I remembered about a man who was dragged to death by a runaway (horse), and for a couple of seconds I thought that could be me.

I fell off. I have to admit this was pure luck. The calf kept running and bucking, looking goofy with the saddle attached to her right side, and the stirrups flipping wild.

I hadn't started hurting yet, not until the next day, but now I started looking around, feeling foolish.

The calf was browsing when I caught up to her, tearing off tall grass with her tongue as big as a purse, a full fat purse – reaching and tucking back as if it is a separate animal – and I wondered if she had forgotten all about the saddle and me riding her. She turned her head, but her eyes said nothing at all, and neither of us mentioned a thing while I uncinched the saddle and took it off. I got it back in the barn, and nobody knew, nobody found out at all.

So, Roxie.

Grandma Mary Belle gave this box and everything in it to Papa long ago, for safe-keeping and remembrance. I think Papa never looks in it. But now you are older, Mama says, you may. Christine and George and I come to the table; we are to sit quietly. Mama has scrubbed the table of all crumbs, all stains of beet juice, and dried it with a towel, and I dried it some more, and then we waited while the air did the rest.

Our hands. Mine are balled up, resting on the table. I look like I will fight somebody, but that's all wrong, so I open them like starfish and lay them down once more. Christine's hands. George's are tapping with his fingers. Mama's hands are work hands and bumpy. This feels like waiting for Easter breakfast.

"Be peaceful," says Mama, and we mostly are, except George's left leg is bouncing up and down. Mama lifts the lid, and we see the sword on top and Grandpa's uniform folded underneath. Mama says, Don't lift them out, I'll do that, but we touch them. George says Please and Mama says Careful, and he lifts the long blade in its sheath. Between them, he and Mama slip the sheath off. There was blood on this sword, says Mama. This is hard to imagine, but we believe it. It is rusty now; it's too bad, even Mama thinks so, but swords are supposed to rust, even though in the War they sang that *thy gleaming sword shall never rust*. Mama says we are to pretend that those words mean more than one thing, and the other thing they mean is the Right and the Good shall never rust.

We have no need of a sword now, but we all like it.

When Grandpa went off to find Lee, *his* Papa gave him two hundred dollars, and most of that went to his uniform: so expensive! He bought the fine grey wool, and took it to someone in Richmond who knew exactly what the uniform was to be: wide pant legs with a dark stripe down each outside, and a coat down to the knees – "a tunic," says Mama, with two long rows of buttons side-by-side down the front, and a leather belt with a buckle. "He wore boots with this, and when he wore his sword, he attached it to a belt catty-corner across his chest from his right shoulder down to his left waist."

Mama sits at the parlour organ and starts to play, *Maryland, My Maryland*, the song with the gleaming sword in it. She says, "Grandpa and Great-uncle Jimmy were so sick of this song. At Richmond, when they weren't battling back and forth, the band struck it up. I suppose it was to keep their spirits high. But your Grandpa and Uncle just got disgusted. When they had time, they thought about the peaches at home at Locust Grove. And wine. Pickles. And young chickens.

"Your Grandpa was known to be a fine horseman. During the War, he would sneak home horseback through the lines at night, couldn't let his Mama and Papa or the little ones see him or they would be in danger, so he found a good way to let them know he was still alive. He rode through the trees near the house in the middle of the night and sang *Dixie* as loud as he could. Can't you imagine the family running to the windows, seeking and seeking to see him in the dark? Waving, in case he could see them? Then he'd ride off. To Richmond, or wherever he was. He did this all the length of the war. Their situation was tricky, because the family was Southern living in the North. The plantation was north of Washington, close to Chesapeake Bay."

Papa never speaks of these things.

Christine lines the packets up in front of us – seven of them. Someone has been careful; each package is the exact same thickness as the others. Why are six tied with twine and one with a blue ribbon? Was it a hair ribbon? We untie them, one by one. Mama says we will read the letters over time, there are so many, but reads us one. She asks George to untie the pictures.

I love these. Here is Grandpa, so handsome. How can he be dead? He is young; how can he be Papa's father? I look hard into his beautiful face and feel sorry he cannot see me, doesn't even know I am born. In the photograph, it seems he does not see anyone, he is just being a soldier. Over his coat he wears a sash which Mama says is ceremonial, I don't know what colour, and here is the sword. He stands straight and tall beside a curtain held back with a tasseled rope. His right hand holds the back of a chair, and he's put his cap, that ducks down in the front sort of squashed, on the seat. He touches the handle of his sword. He looks straight at us, not knowing. Under the picture he's written, *Yours truly, G.M.E.* He doesn't know yet that he is George Malcolm the First. Mama doesn't know who he gave the picture to, to be saying "Yours truly," which is not what you say to your family. On the back, he signed it again, and underneath is where he is.

VANNERSON
Photographic Artist
No. 77 Main St.,
RICHMOND, VA.

Right in the middle of a war.

The second picture was taken in a studio too. It is of Grandpa with four other men. They all wear that uniform. Mama says they are the officers of Libby Prison, a horrible place that before the war was a pork-packing factory or maybe one that made drinking glasses. Grandpa is an intelligence officer, which doesn't just mean he was smart, and the Warden. Grandpa kept people prisoners. The man behind him is Captain Todd, Mrs. Lincoln's brother, which makes him the enemy of his sister! Mama says it was like that. It is like that, in wars.

Grandpa is the most handsome. He is so, so handsome. Here, forever and ever, he is younger than Papa.

This letter is to Dora, who was eighteen.

Richmond
April 5, 1863

Dear Sister,

I have just arrived and avail myself of a certain opportunity by which a letter will reach you.

My long silence may be accounted for from this fact: I never like to write and have letters not reach their place of destiny, which would probably have been the case if I had written before.

Since I last wrote I have been in several skirmishes, and one *long race* with the enemy. The skirmishes were not *very* pleasant, but the race was delightful, 26 miles in length. The Yanks, as usual, gained the race, to both their sorrow and delight. They ran like a flock of sheep, and our men like a set of wolves, after them. Twice they came to bridges when the water was many feet below, and in the anxiety to get over, each man did his utmost to get ahead of his leader. Consequently, numbers were thrown into the water below. At every jump their horses made, our men were behind shooting, cutting and sticking Mr. Yank in the back, and they, *poor creatures*, only using their heels and spurs as modes of defence, holding on either to the pummel of the saddle, or mane, with both hands. They seemed to have especial revenge against the poor horse. He was the only thing they used any weapons against, while their Revolvers and Sabres were quietly reposing in their respective holsters and scabbards. The scene was amusing and ridiculous in the extreme. At last our men moved with compassion on the distressed and terrified foe. Only dashed in among them, seized the revolvers and led Mr. Yank to the rear. Had you have seen the race you would have died with laughter. We passed through two towns where there were a great many ladies who ran into the street, amidst the excitement, cheering the men on, in many instances embracing the horses. And in every instance where the rider dismounted, he was sure to be very affectionately received.

My Company behaved splendidly. Captured a great many and killed several. Two of us, a member of Company C. from Baltimore (Mac Shorb) and myself charged on a party of (8) Yanks, captured (7) and ran the (8th) into his Regt. which was four miles from where we first started the party. I, having the best horse, and decidedly the fastest, did the capturing while Mac took charge of them. You, no doubt, saw an account of it. The Yanks, for a wonder, confess a "great defeat."

I am now recruiting to raise the Battalion to a Regiment, as it is, it is as large as some Regiments on the field. My Company is quite large, next to the largest in the Batt. and decidedly the finest looking and best drilled and disciplined in the whole Brigade. I have now 90 splendidly mounted men.

I'm sorry to know Miss Kate Hyatt has married a Yankee. It seems all the girls in Maryland are taking advantage of our absence and getting married to the first handsome face who proposes, laying aside politics. None of us can ever have any regard for any lady who would lower herself to be wedded to a Yankee. Give my love to all the family, and write often. I am tired of doing all the writing. I will again before I leave. Address me Co. B 1st Md. Cav. Md. Line.

Your affectionate Bro.

George

This is in the blue poems book. Mr. Walt Whitman wrote it:

Two together!
Winds blow south, or winds blow north,
Day come white, or night come black,
Home, or rivers and mountains from home,
Singing all time, minding no time,
While we two keep together.

*

"Christine, Grandpa is my lover."

"Then you cannot call him Grandpa."

"Then George. Like George. Like Papa. Oh dear. What shall I call him?"

"A love-name. Like Beloved, like Dear One."

"Yes, and when I grow up, I will marry someone who looks exactly like him. And is strong. Strong as he is. And bold."

"You're not grown yet; you will probably change your mind before then."

I am sure I will not.

Mama says Grandpa didn't like it there, at Libby Prison – thousands of prisoners coming in every week – and neither did James William; they both wanted to go out and find Lee. After a year or maybe some longer, Grandpa was free to join the First Maryland Cavalry, Company B, and he was in heaven, says Mama, a young man's heaven, so crazy about horses, so born to chase, to ride for miles and days and with little rest. He mostly loved the War, even though he was captured once (but he stabbed the guard and got away, and this just down the Baltimore Pike from his home).

Then came Gettysburg. Grandpa's Rebels had to retreat from there, and then, Mama says, came the unspeakableness of Monterey Pass. There, all was in pitch blackness, and the rain was thunderous.

Grandpa and his men wore black gum blankets over their uniforms, trying to stay dry. That was a good thing, because General Custer's men came upon them and did not recognize they were Confederates. Grandpa's Company shielded their one cannon from sight with their bodies wrapped in their blankets until the last minute and then stood aside and shot straight into the enemy, charged them then, and drove them down the mountainside. Grandpa says, "the shouting and the firing among the retreating enemy – we concluded that they had become panic-stricken and were accidentally fighting among themselves."

The darkness was darkest anyone could imagine. They were so high in the mountains that they could hear the roar of thunder and see lightning flashing *below* them. The rain poured and poured. Little streams turned into torrents. It was so horrible, and some Rebels, not Grandpa's, gave themselves up, saying the War was not worth it.

The Union soldiers were fooled, thinking there were more Confederates than there were. Grandpa's men, who were only twenty, and with only one cannon, held off seven thousand Union troopers for over five hours. But then they could not resist any longer, and, after the whole battle was over, one thousand Rebel soldiers were prisoners. Grandpa had been shot and shelled and cut with a sabre. But he was alive.

Otherwise, I wouldn't be here, none of us, except Mama.

*

Papa, what is a gum blanket?

Papa looks and sees me and my question. "Juanita, it is just a blanket like any blanket, probably made of wool, but it has been soaked to make it proof against the cold. The rain. Soaked in resin collected from a tree – "

Papa knows I have been looking in the box. He says quietly, " – like a soldier might need, in a war."

Report of James H. Lane, Brigadier General, C.S.A.

I understand from official report of the commanding officer of the 18th Regiment, North Carolina troops, that General A.P. Hill, Staff and couriers were in the road, in advance of the 18th at the time, and to avoid the enemy fire, some of them dashed into the woods, over the 18th, which fired into them, mistaking in the dark for enemy cavalry.

After this unfortunate mistake, I received information that a body of troops was moving on our right. I at once sent Lieutenant (J.W.) Emack and 4 men to reconnoiter and they soon returned with a Pennsylvania Regiment, which had thrown down their arms and surrendered themselves prisoners of war.

When the enemie's artillery opened upon us again, I at once sent the Regiment to the rear under Captain (J.P.) Young, his company having been detailed as a guard, and turned over Lieutenant Colonel Smith, Commander of the Pennsylvania Regiment, to Captain (R.H. T.) Adams, Signal Officer, to be taken to General A.P. Hill.

I shall always feel proud of the noble bearing of my brigade in the battle of Chancellorsville – the bloodiest in which it had ever taken part – where the 33rd discharged its duties so well as skirmishers, and the 18th and 28th gallantly repulsed two night attacks made by vastly superior numbers, and where the 7th and 37th vied with each other as to who should first drive the vandals from the works.

Its gallantry has cost it many noble sacrifices and we are called to mourn some of our bravest spirits. The fearless (T.J.) Purdie was killed while urging forward his men; the gentle but gallant (J.L.)

Hill after the works had been taken and Johnny Young, a mere boy, not yet 18, but a brave and efficient Captain, fell at the head of his company. Captain (W.J.) Kerr, Lieutenants (E.M.) Campbell, (R.A.) Bolick, (J.W.) Emack, (J.W.) Weaver, (J.W.) Bouchelle, (Wm. K.) Babb, (J.D.) Callais, and (Charles C.) Ragin all fell in the gallant discharge of their duties, as did also J. Rooker Lane, of Company E 5th, Virginia Cavalry, who at the time was acting as my volunteer aide.

May, 1863

Please read the letter...

Margaret is dressed for the afternoon. She paces from the window to her chair, chair to window to chair; abruptly sits, rocks: forward and back, forward and back; she begs, Please read the letter – this time, Lydia, oh read what they *really* say – between the lines, please. Read that this *Regret to inform you*...it is code to say he is coming home, home through the lines, home...

...Lieutenant James William Emack fell at Chancellorsville the day after he and his four-man patrol heroically captured and returned to the 7th North Carolina, Confederate States Army, the entire 128th Pennsylvania Regiment. Regret this delay in informing you, Sir and Madam, as General Thomas J. Jackson was shot almost immediately afterward. In the confusion...

...home, because soon it will be time for the peaches, James, peaches, and there will be young chickens. And what of Ned? He is but four, James, and every day waits for you to come home.

*

This is what they do.

Young men, dead on the field of battle, are found with coats unbuttoned, shirts ripped open, trousers torn askew, half off. These are not the violations of the enemy, or of animals. They have done this themselves, to see their wounds, where they have been wounded. They know by now that if they have taken wounds to their organs, they will die.

*

Margaret takes to riding in the mornings – down the long lane from the house to the Baltimore and Washington Turnpike. She saddles up young Jezebel. Margaret's great impulse is to kick Jezebel into a gallop, but instead she shortens the reins. The sun, even at this early hour, even filtered by the locusts lining the lane, is a fierce blaze. The red clay glares up at them.

This first day, when she reaches the Pike, she dismounts and looks into the south – to Washington, eight miles away, enclosed these two years within massive fortifications and earthworks. But it's beyond. She urges her soul to go farther – to the forests, the dark woods around the Chancellor house.

The air on her face is hot, the leaves on the trees do not move. No one is nearby, only Jezebel and God. She speaks softly, soothingly, to Jezebel, for she will scream now.

Her screams come forth in a frantic, rasping whisper. JAMES! JAMES! JAMES!

She hears herself: I am a madwoman. She weeps until she is empty.

For days this is her custom. She sends her voice far into Virginia: JAMES! JAMES! JAMES! Her voice will revive him.

One morning, she feels an unexpected anger, even a fiery edge of rage, that he does not reply. It frightens her.

On the last day, she dismounts and lies down on the rough ground: her cheek here on home ground: oh, James's cheek...She calls him again, Jimmie...her voice finally tired. When she gets to her feet, she presses her face into Jezebel's warm, muscular neck, and tells her this is the end of it.

Margaret assures her parents, who do not believe her, that she is doing well. The others – Charlie, Frank, Johnnie, Dora, Ned – who have seemed all these days as insubstantial as ghosts, take on flesh and features again. Elbert is heartbroken, and her sheltering tree.

*

George has written to Dora. A Mr. Spallen, of Virginia, knows of our family. When he heard that James had been killed, he retrieved his body and buried him in Virginia.

*

It was years before we could thank the Spallen family, years before we could bring James home. We buried him with the Emacks in the Episcopalian churchyard across the Pike. We carved his headstone with a broken pillar grown over with ivy and roses. We carved his name and whose son he is, and Elbert chose Jeremiah 48:17:

All ye that are about him do bemoan him
and all ye that know his name, say, How
is the strong staff broken, and the beautiful rod!

We erected an iron fence around his headstone, as if to say we can protect him.

I know he is there. Still, before I stop myself, I call to him – lying in the woods near the Chancellor house.

Grandpa wrote this from Shepherdstown, Virginia, on July 21, 1863. It's to his sister, Eudora, who is home at Locust Grove.

My dear Dora,

You no doubt heard that I was wounded at Monteray, Pa., in a cavalry fight, and in all probability, my condition has been exaggerated. I was wounded in five places – shot through both arms and right hand. Also was struck with shell on my right knee and leg. Those wounds were more painful than either of my arms. It was a week before I could walk without the assistance of someone, and had to be assisted on and off my horse as if I were a child. I am now happy to say I am almost well. My hand entirely well and my arms are recovering rapidly. I was very severely bruised with sabre cuts over my shoulders and arms, which have not entirely disappeared. I thought at the time (excuse the expression, more appropriate than refined) that I was about to "go up the spout," but was protected by providence, I believe. I lost a great many men in the fight, so many killed, wounded and missing. Billy, Dick and Dolly are among the latter. I had 210 men protecting a wagon train against cavalry and artillery force. We held them in check until all our ammunition had given out. The Yankees charged us, as soon as they found out that was the case, and captured about 30 wagons. Had it not been for the cowardice of two regiments who came to my assistance, then turned and ran at the first fire of the Yankees, I would not have had as many taken prisoner, nor a wagon.

General Jones, who was in command, complimented me very highly before the whole command. General Ewell also complimented us in beautiful language.

I only regret the most gallant men of my company their suffering. Such is always the case.

At the Battle of Gettysburg we lost a great many soldiers. We have the consolation of knowing that the enemy loss was very much heavier.

I have just returned from across the river where I convalesced in safety. My friends, Miss Alice S., P., W. – destined for their homes. I *pray* they may cross in safety. They are such lovely girls. I know you would like them so much if only you knew them. Which I hope you will soon. I delivered them safely to Major —— of the 1st Md. Cavalry, who made me the promise to take good care of them. This is one of the most delightful places in Virginia.

Poor McLeod Turner was very badly wounded and left on the Battlefield at Gettysburg. He was wounded in both legs and through the body. I fear he will not recover. You know he is our cousin.

Calder and Louis escaped unhurt, I am happy to say. McLeod is now Major and has been since poor Jimmie's death. Mr. Spallen (?) had Jimmie's remains recovered and placed in a Chancellorsville cemetery. He died doing his duty.

The day before he was killed he took, with the assistance of four men, an entire Regiment of infantry prisoners. This seems almost marvellous, but nevertheless true. He was complimented by his Col. and Gen. for his gallantry. Next day, he was shot.

I wish God to have taken me in his place. It breaks our hearts, but all is done for the best. Poor Jimmie was prepared to die, and I am not. I trust I may meet Jimmie in heaven, should I be worthy of so divine a place.

I saw Dr. Hunter a day or two since. He was looking remarkably well. I heard from Maggie not long since. They are all well and very anxious I should come to Tenn. to see them. Uncle James and family are well. If Cousin Alice knew I was writing she would send her love. Tell Aunt May the Major looks splendid. Give my love to Mother and all the rest of the family. To Aunt Martha, Uncle Tom, and all my relatives...

I did report for duty but Major Brown had me taken off my horse and sent me to a hospital again. Write to Miss Nannie, and she will forward all your letters to me. I have not heard a word from home since last November. I received hearsay greetings from you sent by Lieut. Johnston...

Give my love

George

*

Papa points out that Grandpa does not refer to his father at all. It is undoubtedly to protect his father from being arrested and interrogated by the Union officers again, suspicious he collaborates with the enemy.

Shepherdstown, Va.
July 23, 1863

My dear Miss Emack,

Any communication you may wish to have with your brother, Captain George Emack, please send to me, I will be very pleased to forward to him, as we have more frequent opportunity than I suppose you have. Although he was here but four days, we all had become so fond of him, that it was with the greatest *reluctance* we let him leave us.

His wounds improved very much, while he was here, and when he left were much better. I only wish it had been in my power to have relieved him entirely.

I know you will pardon me for writing this *free unceremonious* note, but I feel like I knew you. Your brother talked so much about you, but I trust it will not be long before we do meet in better times. Hoping to hear from you *very soon*, let me subscribe myself,

Your true friend,

Nannie McEndree

If any of his *friends* wish to write, they can send in the same way.

Dalton, Md.

July 24, 1863

Dear Madam,

It is with pleasure that I write to assure you of the good health of your son, Captain Emack, of the Maryland Battalion of Cavalry. He left us on Monday evening, July 13 to cross the river at Williamsport.

A few moments before he left he gave us your address, requesting me to write you. You may have heard of him having been wounded in a fight at Monterey (Pa) on the night of the fourth, while guarding a wagon train.

When he left us he was rapidly recovering from his wounds, which were flesh wounds, and though painful were not dangerous. He was wounded in both legs, and had several sabre cuts on his back. He was with us from Friday the 10th until Monday evening.

When he first came he seemed weak from the loss of blood, and a little stiff when walking, and required some little assistance in mounting his horse, which I assure you was a splendid animal, captured the night he was wounded.

The left arm was still almost useless to him but nothing could dampen his spirits. He was in fine spirits and was quite annoyed with me for saying General Lee had the worst of the fight at Gettysburg.

He was in need of nothing that I could discover. He would have written you himself, but he left Maryland sooner than he expected.

If I have not been sufficiently particular and there are any questions you wish to ask, it will give me pleasure to answer them.

The Captain desired me to say that immediately after the battle of Chancellorsville he wrote you of his brother (Lt. James William), who was killed in that battle, and he was afraid you never received it.

His brother was attached to the 9th North Carolina. The particulars of his death he did not give me, it seemed so painful for him to speak of his brother.

Yours sincerely,

Luddu Dallz
Williamsport
Washington County, Maryland

The enclosed piece of paper he also gave me, desiring that I should tell you of his cousin, Major McLeod Turner, who was dangerously wounded and left on the Battlefield of Gettysburg. He desired that I should tell you of his cousin, and I know one line from an absent son is highly valued. (The note is on the back of a torn off corner of a letter dated May 5, 1863, York, Pa. M.T.E.)

There's a sound of a terrible tumult at the river. I hear it before I can see it. Roxie and I are soaking wet; it's been raining hard for an hour. More than an hour. Mrs. Dillon suggested I stay until this storm passes over, but I need to get home. Then I see it, the edges, frothing, they're so bashed and crashed on the land, and on land the normal banks are gone. There are even limbs of trees out there in the middle, tearing along, not catching on anything because everything is under all that water.

Roxie, let's go.

*

It was when the bridge was swept away, when Big Old Piney was furious and churned brown over her banks. When I had gone to town with eggs and cream before it started, and had to get back because Mama said, "Come straight home." It was when I held Roxie's head firm and urged her into the water, to step in and *swim...* It was when Roxie got out into the stream, and I could feel all that huge water pushing us, carrying us sideways, and Roxie keeping her head to the other shore, and me holding her tight to the bit – it was then that I felt my veins fill up with George Malcolm.

My company is next to the largest in the Batt. and decidedly the finest looking and best drilled and disciplined in the whole Brigade. I have now 90 splendidly mounted men.

Always, thinking about Grandpa, as if he was my faraway sweetheart, and we each other's age. Of course I made that up, and shouldn't have, I know it; he is Papa's father, and by now if he was alive would be very old, and Grandma's sweetheart and husband besides, but

I couldn't help it – I felt like that. But now was different.

Since I last wrote I have been in several skirmishes, and one long race with the enemy. The skirmishes were not very pleasant, but the race was delightful, 26 miles in length... The Yanks, as usual gained the race, to both their sorrow and delight. They ran like a flock of sheep, and our men like a set of wolves, after them...At last our men moved with compassion on the distressed and terrified foe. Only dashed in among them, seized the revolvers, and led Mr. Yank to the rear.

This George Malcolm coursed into my arms and legs, right into my heels, pushing firm into Roxie's sides and up my backbone into my mind where I felt him in my eyes, and I felt his intentions were the same as mine, and my intentions were that we were going to reach the other side, me and Roxie, and even if we got pushed sideways and downstream, we would not be swept away.

*

I start to shake after I tell Mama. She says, "It's like that; you're steady and after you're safe you're not – tell me about Roxie again."

So I do, how Roxie was a warrior and not a spoiled brat. She was a Roxanne. She kept steady to the far shore.

Mama says, "I'll rub your shoulders," and I say yes, but then they hurt too much and so do my arms, and Mama says, "Lightly, lightly, I'll do it lightly." And she puts on the big kettle and she makes me a bath.

"I regret, Juanita, that I didn't qualify 'Come straight home.'"

The water is so good. I feel my back long, growing straight up out of my tailbone like a cottonwood. The word 'spineless' pops into my head, a word of disgust I've heard, and I think, I'm not, I've got one, and it makes me laugh. Mama turns around but I don't tell her what *... I have a spine like Grandpa.*

*

It did me good. Since that day I have joined the boys' baseball team. They have wanted me all along, because I can run faster than any of them, everyone knows it, but until I went through the flood it didn't enter my mind to join, and nobody asked me to. But after, with Grandpa in my veins, it has just happened naturally.

Nobody objects, even though at school the boys are kept over there, and we girls over on the other side, but nobody raises the subject. I am just the best runner. Even when I have to hold up my dress in one hand.

George isn't especially interested in running. He practices pitching, day after day. He gets one of the other boys to catch, and he pitches and pitches until the boy's hands sting too much. Overhand. He's good. Our family is known as good ball players. George throws and I run.

*

Our country is at war. With Germans. One of the Mirrills is going.

TRACKS

It snowed in the night. How smooth the world is! The little ones will make angels; maybe I will show them how, but they already know in words, because Christine told them. Oh, *I* will make an angel!

My job is to get some old harness from the barn. Papa will show me how to cut it to make new soles for my shoes. We have a metal last; I will cut and glue and he will do the sewing, because his hands are stronger than mine, bigger.

But the snow...here are tracks, heading across the sorghum field. They go as far as I can see, and they are not the horses', they are not a rabbit or groundhog, more like a dog's tracks. Whose? The snow isn't deep, but it comes over my shoes, but by now I really want to know about this dog, so I follow and follow, clear across the field into the next. Tracks, tracks. A big hazelnut ahead, and then this! The track goes this way around the tree and *also* that way around the tree! I remember – a prairie wolf will do this, go ahead, and his friend or relative will step exactly in his tracks behind. This is why Teeley says he is a trickster. She says we mustn't take him lightly; he is a hero among creatures and has power. So I follow the easterly track as the other wanders off to the west. I am starting to think about getting the harness for Papa, but keep going until the tracks come up to a stand of red-barked dogwood, *very* red, especially against the whiteness, and here! one set of tracks goes to the left, another to the right.

I start to think this means there are at least three of them, maybe more, and I am only one.

I turn around and walk home fast. I never once saw them.

George came in the night. Griff heard him first, in the darkness of the orchard, challenged him, and was about to attack with his stick, but then George laughed. Laughed and didn't call out or knock; he simply walked into the house. Elbert made a sound as if he had been struck in the chest, and staggered from his chair to embrace him and I thought he would never let him go, George laughing and laughing.

I cannot bear to look at him. Not for the density of whiskers on his jaw – he must shave – but for the almost incandescent glow of health upon his cheeks and brow. How wrongly handsome he is, how indecently alive he is, and James – James's bones dissolving into someone else's land in Virginia. That George, too, is heartbroken acts on me in a reverse way. How dare he? He so alive, so relishing this war, his great adventure, what right?

I am insane.

He sits beside me on the sofa, its dark brown horsehide stuffed with horse hair. There! Like a horse, yes, but dead, dead. How confident he is as he takes my hand. With all my might I resist pulling it away. I am changed.

His trouser leg: grey, worn. His moustache. Thick and brown. Emack hair. In spite of myself, I glance to his eyes. They are tender. He is not insane. He fathers me, me insane. He knows good things about being a man. But I am far inside.

Next day, before he leaves, we sit outdoors and read the letters from James that George has not seen. We stop often, so strong are our thoughts. George reads, I read, out loud to each other, and it is difficult: out loud. But very good. To hear James.

Now he is gone, into the dark, cantering south and east across the fields. I wish I had stroked his moustache, kissed his face unreservedly.

James's letters are badly bent, and whole words, sentences and segments are indecipherable. Still, we read what we can see, and make up the rest.

Richmond
July 21st, 1862

Dear Mother,

It has long before this time in...(2 p.m.) occurred to you that this is the anniversary of the battle of Manassas...no doubt it seems like a long year and to the men (?) who are flying fugitives over the land very long and this...is crowded with many of that class...it seems to be the place of refuge, even when besieged, but thanks to Divine Providence...and our brave soldiers it is now relieved of that state, but to all appearances only temporarily, one year ago it liked to have been in same situation, what events have transpired since then? I scarce know, for I have hardly thought, they transpire and are almost immediately forgotten, in the great rush and excitement of times, but history will someday come to our aid, whoever are fortunate enough to be among the living, for at the present state of wholesale slaughter but few comparatively will enjoy that privilege; so it will ever be as long as there is an enemy in our land, for their is no diminution in determination...there is in succumbing, it is useless however to waste time speculating upon the future, time alone will develop our destiny.

I wrote you on the 7th inst. and think it very probable that you will, or have received it; this will go by a friend that you once knew, I think he put the first threshing machine...that I recollect seeing in operation on Father's place. I think he also will be successful in getting through. As I stated in my letter of the 7th I had just returned from Charlotte, N.C. where I had been about 8 weeks, so far as comfort goes...arrangements were not pleasant, for this place is so crowded, it is with great difficulty you can get lodging or board; I was fortunate...to get in with Major...H. and Mr. W., Mrs. W. being in Columbia, S.C. for the present; if they had not taken me in, I suppose I would have to have done like some others are doing, viz bunk in...All three of my kind friends are well, we expect Mrs. W. back in a few days when I will have to vacate; but I shall depend upon my usual good luck, for another place.

I have seen a number of our friends lately, McLeod was here too since on his return from a pleasure trip up the country for the benefit of his health, he was very much improved by it, and now has joined his regiment, about 4 miles from town. I saw Thos...a few days before, was looking very well indeed, desired me to send his love to you all when I wrote, he would like very much to hear from you all; a soldier's life seems to use him well, he was at nearly all the battles around Richmond but escaped...captured some fifteen or twenty Yanks himself, they seem very willing to give up and be taken. I have seen a number of them when they were brought in, and could scarcely help pitty...they were so humble and obedient. I also saw Calder a few days since, he was complaining slightly from the effects of a shock produced by the explosion of a shell that killed the man next him, and scattered the fragments all over C., but no portion of the shell struck him. I gave you a full description of it in my...I spent yesterday evening with Geo and Dolly C. both of whom are at the prison. Geo looks rather the worse for hot weather and a good...of fatigue, that he has gone through since they have been bringing Yanks in so rapidly. I think they have now about 10 thousand. He has written several times lately; he sent one by a... major, and an...with 100 in it, the major was to send by express to Washington, D.C. and send the Express Co.'s...by mail. Dolly is looking very well, thinks it is a hard case...hear from home, is in good spirits, is very well satisfied with a soldier's life. Billy W. has joined the Maryland line again... here a few days since.

Uncle James and family are well, he wrote to Grandma when here a few days since, she writes in excellent spirits, is so anxious for me to come out, and try my luck with a 30 thousand...I am afraid I will have to decline, as a furlough is out of the question now. Aunt H's crops are very fine...the neighbourhood all send their love, Aunt D's health is very good. Major A.E. Jackson called to...will, and if they don't like that let them stop it or come...I am the responsible party, they will get their share of trials and troubles of this war before it is over...I trust; I sometimes think I ought to save myself with that particular object in view; miserable wretches they know but little of the vengeance that is stored for them here; I trust they will feel it full force some day, war is better than peace for them. I only heard that Father was arrested and released today, heard none of the particulars except that it was because they thought he was carrying on a correspondence with G...here; I know they could not prove that as neither of us have addressed a line to him, neither have we received a line; as you are all noncombatants, I hope they will see no further necessity for making their unwelcome visits; they tried to make us a visit here, several times, but have unavoidably been prevented doing so, very much to their regret, but no doubt they are determined to make another effort, and henceforth there will be numerous retreats...more defeats and c. and c. their veracity I presume no one doubts for a moment, and we are doomed.

I have just returned from dinner, where I found Mrs. W...returned this morning; you can say to our friends when you see them, that they are all well, also give my love to them all.

How has Aunt M's western fever gotten, I reckon she has almost given up in despair; tell her she may as well make herself contented until the war is over, which perhaps is not very...off; she had better eat peaches this summer and get fat, I expect you have plenty of them; if you were down here you would know how to appreciate them, if there are plenty Geo and I will take our share in cans next Christmas, or some other, but don't let them go the way of mince meat, if we should happen to be delayed, tell Aunt I not to forget the pickled...and wine; a few spring chickens would also come in well. I mention these things as I have an unusual appetite for our delicacies at this time. I will try and keep them in memory... breast I would like to hear how sister is progressing but if I...can't so will have to put up with it and refer her to some of my old letters for advice if she wishes any. I hope she is improving in her music, but I have to request that she will drop *Maryland, My Maryland* for I never was so thoroughly disgusted with any tune in my life, it seems to me I hear nothing else wherever I go, it has worn out entirely, except with the darkies.

Tell Father, I am astonished that his friends should have suspicioned him, of traitorous doings, he had better cut their acquaintance (I suppose he has no objection to receiving a message from his rebellious son occasionally) and take no further notice of them.

I believe I have told you all the news, I can't think of any more now, at any rate, so I must close with an affectionate adieu to you all.

Your Affec...e Son J.

*

We cannot bear to leave James's letters, George and I, and George picks up the first one and starts reading it once more. How clear his voice is!

Richmond, Va.
July 7, 1862

Dear Mother,

I arrived here last night after a stay of two months in Charlotte N.C., one of the most pleasant places I ever was in, enjoyed myself very much, and although upwards of two hundred miles farther south, it is at least ten degrees cooler than here. While down there I made Uncle James a visit...distance of about 40 miles from C. found all well and on my return here saw Martha Daisy and Miss Emily...at the depot, all were well but in a great deal of anxiety about Calder McLeod and Thomas P. all of whom have come out of the several days' fighting without a scratch so far. C. came within an ace of being killed, the regiment was lying down receiving the enemy's fire, when one of...shell struck the man lying next him, exploded...i him to pieces, and covering C. with the human fragments and so much stressed him that he was carried from the field, supposed to be dead but he soon recovered and has been with his regiment ever since. McL is...being too much worn out to remain on the field, and is suffering from an attack of diarrhea. Thomas G. is also with the regiment and is well. You may perhaps have heard or may yet hear that...H. was killed but it is not so, he is still among the living and unhurt although his death was published. Dolly C. has been here sometime assisting G. at the prison. I saw him this morning, looks very well, says he has not heard from home for a long time...arrived here a day or two since after a long tramp to avoid the Yankees in the valley, he was with Jackson but in some way got lost from his regiment during one of the engagements, and was left in the enemy's lines, and is supposed to have been taken prisoner; they came very near getting him as it was. I suppose you have heard of the death of Lieut. Nich.s Snowden by this time, he was killed but a month since in the valley, not being here at the time I did not hear the particulars. The battle around Richmond has been the most terrible ever fought on this continent and has resulted in driving the enemy to fifteen miles below on the James river, where he is again under the protection of his gunboats, with which the river now swarms. The boats have saved the Yankee army from utter ruin; as it is we have broken every one of their fortifications, with the guns in...was done with immense loss at the point of the bayonet. We also have some seven or eight thousand prisoners and they are still being brought in. We have a great number of their wounded and several complete batteries. Stonewall Jackson got completely in their rear and...them on this side of the Chickahominy. McClelland... the bridges to prevent Jackson from following...he was...attacked, and driven from our fortifications...to another, and is now between the Chickahominic and the James, in a kind of peninsular, but for their gunboats they would be captured entire, but the contest is nearly over, it is rumoured the fight was...today.

Last week, the battle commenced on the north side of Richmond and was so near that the musketry could be distinctly...the flash of the cannon distinctly seen from housetops and hills. Our loss has been very great, the city is filled with wounded, and every possible attention is being shown them; it is horrible to behold, but it can't be helped, and we do all that we can to alleviate their suffering; the ladies are untiring in their attentiveness. We have Yankee papers up to the 4th...and know exactly what kind of accounts you get, what I have written you may rely upon, and a call by Lincoln for 300,000 more men would seem to vivify it more than anything else published in their papers.

Geo is well but looks badly, has been kept very busy since the Yankees have been coming in so rapidly, he...and Uncle James wrote a few days since, I hope they will reach you all. Eugene Fairfax was killed in the battle of Yorktown. Carlisle was wounded in one of the late battles but has recovered sufficiently to go to his father's family who are now at Warrenton N.C. I saw Julian several times. Tom Hun...is with his father at Mobile. I think I have not heard a word from home since the middle of March. I would like very much to hear, and do not...an opportunity...paper without writing. This is the first letter I have written since I left N.C.

I expect to remain here until ordered away which I do not expect directly, and will write every opportunity. I have a great deal to say but have not time now. I am well and very comfortable except so far as hot weather prevents. I wrote to Aunt H. and Maggie too while away but did not receive a reply, perhaps G. has heard but I forgot to ask him this morning.

With my love to each and every one I remain
Your Affectionate

J.

The world is dappled and striped with corn and sun and the leaves of corn moving in the wind. The leaves are like swords – some twisted, some bent; some are curled tightly inside each other like scrolls with secrets. Shadows move and make a hundred shades of green – more – and I am in a long hallway of what is green.

I walk to the end, and to the gate. I think the best about any gate in any garden or any place is the other side with the murmurous voice. There is a sound of a question all around its edges and in its latches and hinges too, that invites a person to slowly step through to Something True there, where It is, shining.

This morning there was blood on my sheets. I was amazed to see how deep red it was, and out of myself. I thought the same thought that Christine said she did too, when she was twelve, *Am I a woman now?*

I told Mama and I cried for the stain and for something else. Afterward, I dug a hole and planted a blue-eyed grass I found in the south meadow, for Mama, and to make the side yard beautiful. All that time she and I were both listening and we don't know what it was, exactly.

Lonely is a person's thirteenth year,
Legs slender, tall as a deer,
Speechless,
Trusts woods,
Four-footed things, and moss
And intelligent birds
(Crow, jay) to be her words
Into the next kingdom.

Of course it is a Kingdom, because of God
And because, Mama says, These days
The Woman Rulers are mostly gone.

Grandma Mary Belle is coming and Mama looks frazzled and Papa went out to the barn.

I have hardly heard of her, except for a photograph we have of only her head. Someone has hand-tinted the picture. She tilts her head to one side, with a flower in her hair and a ruffle around her neck. She looks straight at us.

Mama says she was considered the most beautiful girl in Kentucky. "After the War, George Malcolm went to New Orleans. There he met a Mr. Wooldridge who was in charge of the New Orleans port, and who invited him to come home with him to Louisville, Kentucky, to meet the family. That's when Grandpa fell in love with Mary Belle who was only sixteen, and she fell in love with him. Her parents said she was much too young to marry, and so they eloped!"

Eloped! I think it is a scandal, and look to see what Mama thinks. She carries on. "Your grandfather was considered for the job of ambassador to Mexico, but he never went; instead, he and Mary Belle were given a plantation, and raised horses. You can imagine how happy that made him."

Anyway, Mary Belle is coming, and Grandpa is dead, and she is coming with an Irishman named Mr. McIlhaney who is her husband now. Already I don't like him, and neither does Mama, I can tell.

*

Grandma looks very tired and not so pretty anymore. She was joyful to see Papa, and held him a long time, and looked in his face, and held him some more.

She was even more joyful to see Uncle Ed, and she teased him, in a sisterly way.

She was honoured and happy to meet Mama and us children.

*

We have nothing to give them. That is why they came, to beg Mama and Papa for money. Mr. McIlhaney had many good and hopeful ideas of how some money could "set them back on their feet," as he said, and Papa doesn't believe any of it, and wouldn't be lured into giving money even if we had some, which we do not. Grandma cried and cried even while she was ashamed of it and ashamed to be begging in the first place. I don't know what they will do.

Papa set his jaw and was cold to Mr. McIlhaney, which seemed to upset Grandma more. He said he couldn't assure them that there would be financial help in the future. He looked for help to Mama, and I thought she might say Grandma can live with us, but not him, but she didn't. She drew her chair close to Grandma and didn't say anything.

They are sleeping in Mama and Papa's room. Mama is under the covers with Christine, and Papa is sleeping with George. They will go tomorrow.

*

She is pretty in the picture, and has no troubles that I can see. In the picture she will marry her darling and have two sons and two daughters. She knows nothing of Mr. McIlhaney. She doesn't know that her darling man will die of pneumonia from riding in the animal car on the train with his horses, to keep them calm, on the way to Laurel, to race them.

When Papa was young, she told him that "your father thought the world of Lee, and when Lee died, he wept. He wept because he heard that, as he lay dying, Lee had said, 'Let the tent be struck.'"

*

Mr. McIlhaney spent everything. Grandma inherited two plantations, and he spent everything.

Plus, he wrote a book about his adventures in the Klondike. But he never was in the Klondike.

Mr. Guthrie is inside school, and I am across the road shinnying up the best hackberry tree. There's nothing rougher than hackberry bark except maybe a crocodile, and I'm scraping the insides of my legs, but it's worth it; there are berries up there. They're far up and away out at the ends of the limbs and then out at the very ends of the branches and twigs. I have to stay on the limb so I won't fall, but I can reach and bend the branch in to where I am and start picking. The taste of hackberries isn't much, but I like that they're crunchy; they're fun. When Mr. Guthrie rings the bell, I'll scoot down quick and be in line almost as fast as if I was in the schoolyard.

Tricky thing is to climb and not ruin my candy. I can't put it in my pocket because it's too sticky and I don't want to eat it yet, so I've got my two littlest fingers bent around it.

Papa and Mama made it yesterday, from our cane made into molasses. To sweeten things. That's all we do with sorghum. Some of the neighbours make moonshine. The Hunters, where we grind our cane and cook it, do. Not Teeley's Hunters. One of the Haleses moved to the next county, to get away from the Revenue agent who found out what he was doing, what his whole family was doing.

Mama stood in the yard, and Papa stood near, with gooey molasses, and they drew and folded, drew and folded, until it got paler and paler and thicker and thicker. Then they laid it out on the porch to get hard, which it really didn't.

Christine and I cut it into pieces. That's molasses taffy. Very sticky.

Mr. Guthrie starts ringing. I skin down and catch up with everybody. In line, I go in, past Mr. Guthrie. I do not look at him and I hold the taffy close to my dress on the side opposite, and he doesn't see it.

Inside, I get my idea.

Mean, mean Mr. Guthrie, who twists our arms, is still in the doorway with the bell, and I walk up front calm and as if I'm not doing anything, and I smear my taffy all over the seat of his chair. I don't even hurry. I go back to my desk and look around and nobody has even noticed. I sit down excited and sort of proud.

All of us children are sitting at our places now; now we stand and face the Stars and Stripes and say *Ipledgeallegiancetotheflagofthe UnitedStatesofAmericaandtotheRepublicforwhichitstandsonenation indivisiblewithlibertyandjusticeforall*, like we always do, then pray to *OurFatherWhoArtInHeaven*. Mr. Guthrie says AMEN in a voice louder than anybody, and we all sit down, especially Mr. Guthrie.

I look at his skinny face harder than I have ever looked at anybody. His eyes change from hard-brisk to sort of filmy, and he blinks one… two…The rest of his face doesn't move at all. Now he starts to get up. He slaps his palms flat on his desk and pushes down. His chin pushes out. From here I cannot see anything, but he twists around and takes a look, and it's now he starts to turn colours. White, then pink, and now – red.

"Boys and girls…"

His voice sounds far away, and very quiet. He keeps on talking, but I cannot hear words. My ears are rushing like Big Piney and my heart is banging against my wishbone. His mouth is moving, he sweeps his head side to side, his eyes drill at us, every one, and now he comes to me and stops, and I know that I show.

"Juanita, step forward," and I do. I am important and afraid and curious all at the same time. I do not know what will happen; this is the first time. For a second I feel awful to see the chair, the seat of Mr. Guthrie's pants, which I only half-see, and candy all over everything. His pants are ruined.

Now I am to say I'm sorry. I look at him to see if he means this. How could I be? Then I realize that he means only that I should apologize, so I do. I say, "I apologize."

But this won't do. I am to say I am sorry. I cannot. His face is too close to me and he heckles me, "Juanita, say you are sorry and be done with this."

He is still pale, his lips so thin and they seem to have no blood in them, and I think he doesn't really mean we will be done with this. I won't say it; I am not sorry.

That is why I am staying at home. ("Juanita," says Mama, "who is the brightest in the whole school, who always has top marks, who has always been good...") Mama and Papa talk to me about saying I'm sorry, and when I say I cannot because I am not they stop trying to persuade me. But I feel how worried they are, and nervous, and I don't like being here daytimes when I should be in school. It's queer.

Mama and Papa asked Mr. Ogle to talk to me. He is a truant officer. He rides into the yard and hitches his horse and suggests that he and I walk into Elk Creek to the Post Office. He asks the same. "Juanita, you must say you're sorry so you can get back to school," and I tell him Mama and Papa taught us not to lie, and I am not. I start to say I don't like Mr. Guthrie, but change my mind.

Mama teaches me. She doesn't say much, but Papa feels personal about everything because he is the Head of the County School Board, and because he chooses the schoolbooks. Papa is different from everyone around here; he is a chemist and has an education.

Every day Papa gets more and more upset, but every day I am still not sorry. I don't think I'll ever be, but I wish I was now. Don't I know something? Don't I know that Mama and Papa do not like Mr. Guthrie either? Or respect him? I saw them giving little glances and head-shakes about him.

But I also know they would forbid me. Even though I know I did what maybe they would've liked to. I will never tell them this, they would say, "Juanita, how could you possibly think we would consider such a thing?" I would feel too lonely.

So I work at home. There's almost nothing more to do in the garden. The summer food is canned; Mama and I did it; the sprouts and cabbages and carrots and potatoes are under the boards in the kitchen floor. Yesterday Papa told me to go to the high field, where the black walnuts and hazelnuts are, to pick up the falls, sort them out. He gave me sacks. I did a good job, and had so many sacks that I didn't have to load them too full, and I was able to bring them home by myself.

The loneliness up there is very bad. I feel how I want to talk to Mama and have her understand me.

It's hard sitting here, hanging my legs off the porch. Papa has been ploughing all morning, in the second field. A minute ago he and Old Kate went into the barn. He'll be watering her and rubbing her down. Then...here he comes.

Oh, tall Papa, here I am, your trouble-girl, Juanita Wildrose, me, seeing you come home weary for dinner.

Papa sees me. He straightens up and changes his face to thunder. I am afraid. I have never been afraid of Papa.

"Juanita, you go pick up the falls at the high field."

"Papa, I did. I did it yesterday."

"There are more; you didn't get them all. You take yourself up there after your dinner and complete that job."

I don't know how to stop myself. I am doing this terrible thing. I am looking at Papa in the face and I am saying, right this minute, I don't even want to, "Papa, I won't."

It is now that Papa turns and tears the branch off a tree. He thrashes me. He holds me by my arm and I cannot get away, and he beats me and he beats me. Mama is here. She sees everything; she calls him and she tries to stop him, but he doesn't hear, and he beats me until he is tired.

*

Mama helps me wash. We take off my blouse; my shoulder hurts from when I was trying to get away. My skirt is dirty and my stockings too (did I fall?) and one has a tear. Mama helps me wash, right here in the kitchen, with water warm from the stove, and soap, and she washes me like she did when I was little.

I cannot stop crying. That is funny, because I don't feel sad. I don't feel anything, but my chest keeps on jumping and a noise hops up into my throat and my mouth for a long time. Mama says, "Don't cry, Juanita," and I say, "I won't," but my chest and my voice keep crying.

Mama dresses me in Christine's middy blouse and my school skirt and her own stockings. She tells me to brush my school shoes, and I do, and then she puts two new laces in them. Then I sit on a chair next to the table and do nothing. I feel sort of as if I am asleep. I start to wonder where Papa is, and now I feel afraid. And now I can't believe it. I know it isn't a dream, but I hope it is.

Mama comes back into the kitchen. Where was she? She says, "Juanita, I am going to Grandma Mirrill's house, and you stay here and I'll be back as fast as I can. And do not go down to the barn."

Now I know where Papa is and that Mama went down there.

I wonder what will happen. Nothing the same. I sit in the kitchen, in the sun landing on the floor and the table there, and my chair, and don't think anymore at all.

There is a fly in the window, buzzing to get out.

And Mama comes back.

"Juanita, I telephoned Elva's Mama in Cabool. She says she will be so glad to have you stay at their place for a few weeks, just for a little time..."

I look at Mama. She has been crying and she is going to cry again. Her eyes are more sad than I have ever seen – ever – even the miscarriages. She takes a long breath that wavers on the way in, and now it's passed over; she is not going to cry after all.

It is so strange. All the happy things I want are happening: Mary Christine's middy blouse, Mama's stockings, Mama washing my back in lovely slow circles, washing my fingers one by one, and now letting me use her black leather valise from when she went to Cottey College. We pack my underwear in it, and a jacket just in case, and my hairbrush. Toothbrush. And the so-happy things don't feel happy. I don't feel them at all.

"Juanita, I'll come part-way."

George and the twins and Ruth come too; it is fun for the little ones; they run ahead and careen down the hill to the creek and get themselves half-soaked by the time George and Mama and I catch up. The creek is low; we jump it, and head up to the road.

"We'll come as far as Grandma Mirrill's, and then I'll have to go back. But Mrs. Cooper will come to meet you, and it'll only be a little while you'll be by yourself."

Mama is being so careful. She's never before thought much about me walking to Cabool by myself. Everything, everything is different.

I tell Mama I'll be fine. My shoulder hurts but I won't say so. I think about Papa in the barn, and how I am afraid of him, and I cannot think about it, that he hit me and hit me.

"It won't be for long, Juanita. Only a little while, and you have a good time, and be good, and help Mrs. Cooper, and remember you'll be going to school with Elva."

School! All the happy things and I don't feel happy.

Mrs. Cooper has walked fast. I can see her coming when I am hardly past Walmers'. She says, "Elva is going to be so surprised..."

And Elva is, she is very surprised, and we unpack Mama's bag and hang up my jacket when Mrs. Cooper says it's a good idea, and go straight out into the backyard. Mr. Cooper has hung two swings out there, from two tall pines, and we swing until it is time for supper.

*

Four weeks. Now Mama telephones that I am to come home. So I pack and Mrs. Cooper hugs me and I start walking. I meet Mama on the road. She has hitched a ride with Mr. Lewis, and sits on the back of his wagon, only the wagon-bed is gone and she is just sitting on the frame. Mr. Lewis stops his horse, and Mama says, "Get on, Juanita," and I do, and we ride, but it's back the way I came. Mama has brought two boxes. One has my books, and one is filled with my clothes. We drive into Cabool and to the train station. We thank Mr. Lewis and admire his good horse a little bit, and we go in, and Mama buys a ticket to Springfield.

Mama says, "You will stay with Uncle Murray and Aunt Nannie, and you will help with your cousin's baby when it comes."

Too soon! I've only just seen Mama again.

PART THREE

Fear ye not, fear ye not
for with my hand I will lead you on,
and safely I'll guide your little boat
beyond this vale of sorrow.
— SHAKER HYMN

I pay attention to the train.

The hugeness of the car. So many seats, caned like dining room chairs. The sway, the swerves and jerks, and most of all, the sound again and again, clackelack-lack, telling about the metal bars of the track, about the metal wheels, and that the train moves, moves over it. The whistle is a long haa-looo like Mama's conch almost, calling Papa in from the fields.

The man in charge of the car and the tickets – it was his idea to tie my boxes with twine. He tied each one both ways and made a loop on top, then wrapped brown paper around the loop to make a handle. He calls me 'young lady.' I want to smile at him.

The land flows by on both sides. Woods, woods, and now a clearing around a cabin or a second-house, and stumps out at the edge where they'll be pulling them out and making the clearing bigger. A horse runs, runs, as if there's no end; a goat. A whole family comes out of the house and stops; they wave. I look hard at them – mother, father, three girls? – a boy and two girls, and let them see my face, that they will remember me going, no, not to Somewhere, but away, going Away.

I feel it then, the awfulness, but as quickly as I can, I make myself into a story for the waving family. I am a mysterious girl with dark brown eyes and dark hair in a braid down her back. Look, she is a Traveller, on the train into an adventure. For an instant, the vast land before the train opens wide as the mouth of a morning glory.

The family is smaller, smaller, gone. The tracks clack past, faster than I can count. One two three four five six seven eight nine ten, one two...I begin to feel sick.

The ticket man comes with a jar of water, and gestures to a woman, a darky, at the back of the car next to the door. It's from her. I sip and bob my head to her; the smile still won't come forth.

*

Uncle Murray is right there on the broad walk beside the train. Uncle Murray, wearing a blue American Express uniform, his big face with whiskers and a big smile. *Give me those, Juanita*, and he takes the boxes and sets them down, then reaches up two big arms for me, and lifts me down in a wide circle, as if I am a little thing, and it is the first that I feel that everything might be all right. Uncle Murray doesn't look like Mama – Mama is wiry – but he smiles like Mama, his eyes do, and he is Mama's big brother.

It isn't far. Uncle Murray walks fast, one box in each hand. I cannot walk that fast and have to run-walk. I try to look around at Springfield at the same time, but mostly I keep my eyes on the big blue suit and his big shoes. City boots.

*

I purely do not like Aunt Nannie.

Uncle Murray and I get there, to his house, I mean, and it's white and made out of long boards overlapping, and steps – six, seven, eight, up to a wide porch and a dark green door, and the door opens in, and a big woman pushes out the screen door, and I do not like her from right now.

"Take her downstairs," is what she says, and she means me and she is telling Uncle Murray, and he turns around to me and squats down.

"Juanita, your Aunt has made up a bed for you downstairs."

We both duck past her as she holds the door.

The cellar stairs are under the stairs that go up. Uncle Murray goes first. Many steps down, and now a choice to go left or right, and we go right, and there it is, my bed, white. I think Can I? and even the next five minutes will be like forever, and I cannot.

Uncle Murray puts my boxes down.

"There. Come upstairs." O, I will.

This is my family. I never pictured Uncle Murray with all these others. Mildred lives somewhere else, and her baby died being born. Aunt Nannie (now not so big but still holds her mouth tight closed and doesn't look at me). Tom and Harry, living away. Felicity, the littlest, here. Everyone here for supper, to see me.

Everything is too fast for me to make up a story like I did on the train. Fast, all actions and the sounds of forks and knives. I will only sit. The sounds pour all around, and I am in a small dark pocket. The children look at me and one of the big boys says – asks – me something, and I cannot, and he goes back to putting a spoon in his mouth. Uncle Murray is large and quiet.

School. Aunt Nannie is talking about school. Of course, school! I will go to school.

*

That night in the white bed under the low log beams, I dream rushed dreams, fast like blown clouds, as if they pass in a flash by the windows of a train.

Then:

Hello, Teeley. Yes, Teeley.

I hear them moan-ning, Juanita. They are moan-ning.

Come sit, Teeley. Oh, standing is fine.

Nunna Daul Isunyi.

Trail where they cried. Oh, Teeley.

In dreams. They come behind my eyes. First the camps where most of them as died did die. In sickness, the cold, starving. They are…

It is such a long way, Teeley.

*

In the morning, I wake up saying a word: coracle. Today I will look it up. Coracle.

*

"Aunt Nannie, may I look up in the dictionary? A word."

Aunt Nannie looks reddish and accusing. "There is no dictionary in *this* house." She is angry about dictionaries.

There is a boy shouting out on the sidewalk. "Wuxtry, wuxtry!" is what he hollers, and she gives me a cent to run out and catch him and buy a newspaper.

Armistice. The War is over and we won.

*

One thousand and six, one thousand seven, one thousand and eight…I wake up counting and I don't know why and then I do; I am counting the seconds before I can go home. Tears burst into my eyes. I could count years and years of one thousand and one, one thousand and two.

I have the shivers. It's cold.

And when I get up, nobody's eyes will rest on me. She will keep doing what she is doing, she will wipe the table off and she will not look up. She will say, Juanita, there's ironing.

I long for Papa's long breakfast prayer, even a long gloom of Jeremiah, while the porridge gets cold. O delicious cold porridge! O, long prayers, I don't mind.

Maybe Uncle Murray hasn't gone to work yet. I sit up fast and pull off my nightgown, pull on stockings, underpants, and my dress over my head. Buttons.

Uncle Murray is gone, Aunt Nannie's in the kitchen, wiping.

*

The bed is just long enough. I put my bottom on the exact right place and stretch out long on my back. I tighten my stomach and lift myself up to sitting.

Faint, I tell myself, and roll my eyes up into my head so I cannot be so on-purpose, and let go all my muscles. I hardly make a sound as I fall back on the bed. No one upstairs can hear. I sit up. Faint, I say again, and roll my eyes up and fall. Every time I give myself over to gravity and not trying, letting myself fall, fall through space, as if I am a hundred miles up in the sky and falling, falling, the lovely air pillowing me until I land on the bed, beautiful bed, bed like grass at home, oh, how it holds me. Hold me, I say to the bed, and it does.

I do this every day for almost two weeks.

*

Dear Mama,

Please, please, write to me. I miss you too much and the little ones. Is Papa still angry? I have to come home for the Christmas holidays. I cannot stay here. I like Uncle Murray but he is mostly gone and after dinner every day he vomits in the sink.

My school is Phelps Grove School, near Phelps Grove Park, at the end of Jefferson Avenue. The girls wear uniforms. A navy-blue skirt, I have one, and a white middy blouse with a sailor collar and a silky black tie. I need one of those.

I have one friend, Ann. Two, because of my teacher, Miss Craig. I use her dictionary any time I please. It's for all of us. I looked up 'coracle.' This is what it is –

a small, round, or very broad boat made of wickerwork or interwoven laths covered with a waterproof layer of animal skin, canvas, tarred, or oiled cloth. Wales, Ireland and parts of Western England. 1540-50. Miss Craig says 1540-50 means when that kind of boat was first built. She was glad to know what a coracle is. She says it sounds like a currach, also a boat, that she knows about because her family comes from the west of Ireland, where the men are fishers, and they go out to sea in a currach.

Do the children know where I am? Mama, please write me a letter.

Lovingly, Juanita

*

I know Mama sent me away because she thought Papa might kill me.

Still, I know she threw me away.

*

A letter from Mama!

I have it under my pillow. While I am sleeping, there it is, right next to my cheeks all night.

Elk Creek, September, 1918

Dear Daughter,

I imagine that you are fully occupied with school and helping out. Are you glad about your new school? and getting to know Felicity? My brother, Murray, is a good man, a loving man, and I am sure that you find him good to live with. His family is very lucky to have you. I have thought this letter to you many times, and not once has it sounded the way I want it to. Juanita, we will be so happy to see you on a visit as soon as it can be managed. Elizabeth misses you terribly, and on the subject of Elizabeth, she says that when she has to leave home, she wants to go to Japan. I couldn't imagine where she got the idea until she brought me her little Christmas doll from years ago, only three inches tall, dressed in a shiny red and gold kimono with a wide sash which is called an obi in Japan, and painted-on white socks and painted-on black shoes. It was the Christmas Papa and we had a little money. Penny-dolls.

I need not say be good, for you will be. Say your prayers, as we do, and always for you.

Your loving Mama

Dear Juanita,

I'm back to Joplin from home. I didn't find out why Papa did it because he didn't talk about it. Mama doesn't talk about it. But they do to God. Mama has a taking-charge attitude before their night prayers, as if Papa is broken and she's taking him for repairs.

Papa doesn't tease anymore. But, Juanita, he had stopped his funning before that day. Before he hurt you that day, something was happening to him already.

Lovingly, Christine

Dear Sister,

We are missing you very very much. When are you coming home? Mark can jump from the swing. He pumps up to the top and when he comes towards the house he jumps through the air almost to the porch. My new outdoor job is to keep the yard neat. I use the sickle first, then I invented sweeping with the broom instead of a rake. Mark ran in and said Mama, make Libby quit sweeping the yard. But she didn't. But everybody talks about it too much.

Lovingly, Elizabeth

Dear Juanita,

Hello, how are you? Come home soon.

Your brother, George

Dear Juanita,

Roxie grabbed Mark by the arm and threw him through the air. Mark's arm is almost bitten through. The vet sewed him together. He said Lucky Maidie Lewis didn't get here first, she puts soot on everything. He said Compared to Maidie Lewis's cures, gashes and fractured bones are no trouble at all. Come home. Mark was quiet until he started yelling.

Your bro, Geo.

Dear Mama and Papa,

Will Mark's arm stay on? Your loving daughter, Juanita

p.s. Tell Mark all our prayers are doing a lot of good.

Also, Mr. Stewart teaches us chemistry. I wish to become a chemist. Chemistry has a separate language, and a very small change can change everything.

Lovingly, Juanita

Dear Juanita,

I helped Mama fix a trellis for a rose bush. We can plant flowers now because Papa has almost finished digging a well and we won't have to go to the spring with buckets anymore. Mama said you are Wildrose and not only Rose because it is the most beautiful of all the roses, and you were so beautiful when you were born. The dowser came and walked back and forth behind the house. His stick is like a wishbone. It jumped around in his two hands and all of a sudden it yanked his arms straight down to the ground. He said to Papa, Mr. Emack, you are to dig your well right here.

Your loving sister, Libby

Dear Daughter,

I am pleased about your interest in Chemistry. It is at the crux of all that takes place in mankind and in nature, and will unfold much for us in the future. My own interest developed early also. When your cousin Henry and I attended the University of Maryland, we both studied chemistry, but eventually Henry switched to metallurgy.

When I left school, my first job was mixing chemicals at the iron foundry at Beltsville, in Maryland. I did the same halfway across the country, in Wichita, Kansas, and that is where you were born, Juanita.

Your devoted Papa

Dear Mama,

I am fine, school is fine. We girls sing every day, getting ready for *Lady of the Lake*. Why didn't I know *Papa is a chemist?* Why isn't he a chemist now? Why are we farmers? Who is cousin Henry? Tell Papa I thank him for his letter.

Lovingly, Juanita

Dear Christine,

Mama says Papa couldn't be a chemist anymore because the chemicals at the foundry would have killed him. The doctor told him his lungs were delicate. Did you know this? What about the time he worked in the mine at Webb City? Mr. Stewart says that there aren't any women chemists. *I want to be one.*

Love, Nita

Dear Juanita,

Breakfast prayers are longer than they have ever been. Papa intends to teach me and Mark something. He leaves out a lot and just reads the part he wants us to know, about Don't spill your seed upon the ground. Onan. This Bible is teeming with lessons. So *you* be good!

Your brother, George

*

I am surprised that George has written this. It must be true what I've heard, that it is easier being brave on paper than face to face.

*

Dear Christine,

This is my last night's dream. Mama and Papa hang in mid-air like angels, their legs bent up behind them, so their bodies look like check marks. Papa is wearing clean overalls and Mama is wearing her light blue dress. They are looking at me where I am on the porch, thinking; they are, and I am.

Love, Nita

*

She left it on the bed in my room. She says she expects me to wear it. A corset.

*

A corset! There's nothing in the front of me, there's nothing in the back of me. I don't stick out anyplace.

Uncle Murray is a farmer, but Aunt Nannie wants to live in town. So they do. He thinks this is too much house, and what he means is, I can't afford it, which Aunt Nannie knows, but she wants a big house and a verandah and that's what she's got. Every house on this block is big with a front verandah and the house on the corner has one that hugs around two sides, and everybody with a front yard and a backyard with a clothes-line; also, a root cellar like a big mystery bump in the backyard.

Aunt Nannie takes in boarders. I don't pay. Aunt Nannie's brother and her father live here. Do they pay? At the supper table, those three are the main people – Aunt Nannie at the end, with those two left and right. Felicity is little, and next to her uncle. Uncle Murray is a hundred miles away down at the other end. He gives me a wink; I think it's about the three. Then he asks me how are Mama and Papa and Christine and George and the rest. I don't know, but I cannot think how to answer him. I'm starting to imagine them in my mind, and Aunt Nannie's voice from her end says, We haven't heard, and if it wasn't for Uncle Murray's eyes still asking me I would sink.

Dear Christine,

I need money for stockings. Mine have darns all up and down my legs; it's embarrassing. I twine my legs around my chair at school so the darns don't blare out, but they do anyway. Navy blue stockings!

All the girls wear a middy blouse. I'm new and so far it doesn't break the rules that I do not, but soon it will. Besides, I don't want to be the new girl after the Christmas holidays. I *need* a middy blouse. Aunt Nannie says it's too bad Ethel gave hers away. I didn't mention Ethel, did I? She is our cousin, and a bookkeeper at Sloane's Store. Sloane's Store is eight storeys high, and because of this The Human Fly was here last summer.

I wish I had seen him! He climbed up the outside of the store with just his ordinary shoes and nothing underneath to catch him. Downtown was packed with people just waiting for him to fall, but he didn't, and when he got to the top, he lifted up his arms and shook hands with himself. Felicity told me. Everybody cheered and hollered Hooray, and two boys shouted at him to do it again, but he didn't, and some of his relatives down in the street took up a collection.

I have started to deliver milk for Uncle Murray. He pastures a beautiful bossy in the neighbour's yard. She's a Jersey, so lovey-eyed, soft-coloured like toffee, and a sweet nature. Uncle Murray milks her mornings before he goes to work, and at evening, and bottles the milk. I take it around to houses near here, and he pays me one cent for each bottle.

But my worst job (the milk isn't worse!) is collecting shoe money. Christine, around here only Uncle Murray knows how to fix shoes, so he fixes them for lots of people. Sometimes when they come to get theirs, they don't have the money just then. That is all right, says Uncle Murray, but if two weeks go by, he asks me if I'll go out and get it. I want to because – twenty cents, and I get to keep one.

The second time there was a bad surprise. The door opened, and it was a girl in my class. While her mother went to get her purse, we stood stiff, as if we were each one a statue, and didn't speak a word.

I didn't do it, but I daydreamed it later on, that we sat down on her porch steps and I told her we were poor too. "… this skirt, for instance, it used to be Christine's. And my cousin Helen Boswell's before that. Mama took it apart and turned it wrongside out, not so worn, and sewed it back together. But before she sewed it, she dyed it navy blue from the grey it was. What Mama did was pour a bottle of ink into the hot water, and that's how she made it blue…."

I daydreamed this because after the shoe day she never looked right at me, and I never looked right at her.

Lovingly, Juanita

I have been looking around for another place to live. Even though I know I will have a hard time persuading everybody, and even though most houses don't need an extra girl. If I do this now, it may turn out to be a good idea in advance. Tatting is in my plan.

I learned from Rose Martin, one of Mama's three best friends. She lives in Cabool (the other best friends are Ida Anderson and Daisy Mirrill, who is Grandpa Mirrill's daughter, not really our grandpa, but he is old and has a long white beard. Most men wear long beards, but not Papa). Rose Martin brought me a shuttle.

I will take my samples to people's doors. I will take their orders and also find out what kind of families they are. (There again! It doesn't go away. I want to go home to Mama and the little ones and Papa the way he was before.)

Tatting. I make good tatting, so does Christine. Now Felicity wants me to show her how, and I will. I have gotten over thinking how could she possibly have come out of Aunt Nannie, and now she's herself. And Uncle Murray is her father, of course.

Tatting suits Aunt Nannie too. She can't stand me reading (I'm not *doing* anything! and she made me stop) so I have started two-thread tatting, and today I'm teaching Felicity.

"This is how you start." It is Saturday and we are sitting on the front step. Felicity presses into my side and fiddles with my hair. She's got my braid wrapped around her neck like a scarf – ow.

"Look, Felicity, hold the bobbin in your right hand, with your fingers like this, and the thread, hoop it up over your left pointing finger." If I put my hands on top of hers and go through the motions...It's awkward, but here it comes – real lace! Just from us moving our hands in mid-air. Felicity is thrilled; she's made something where there wasn't anything before. Mama must have felt like this, teaching us, waving and weaving, our four eyes on the same place.

I tie up the thread ends and give Felicity the little piece of tatting. There, you made real lace. That's all. We'll do it some more next Saturday. Felicity groans that we're stopping, but runs into the house to show her mother.

My plan is to show the neighbours. I have several widths and several patterns, adding up to eighteen, and I can use black or white thread – thirty-six – and even other colours maybe, although nobody does that, but maybe a deep rose, that would be beautiful. Or even three shades, rose to pink, three shades, emerald to apple green!

My sample card: stiff paper from a box, ten inches one way, eight the other way, with lengths of tatting now snug around it. Five cents a foot, Aunt Nannie thinks, and I agree, and more for wider: eight cents. Take orders. Then after school and chores, I'll tat and make deliveries and collect money.

For bus fare, for one thing.

To go places, get away from here and all her stacks of ironing. She looks crafty when she finds out I'm a good ironer. She goes for more things – old linens, sheets, pillow cases, finger towels, things unused forever, and she washes them and brings them to me to starch and press.

Mama praised me, Juanita, they are lucky to have you, but she doesn't know how it is. I don't feel lucky and neither do they. Uncle Murray, I love him, and Felicity is dear, but everyone else…Aunt Nannie is a witch. If it weren't for her, I'd be glad to iron, because this is an electric iron. It's light to pick up and it's very smooth on the bottom, and I don't have to wrap the handle with anything to keep my hand from burning.

My samples look very handsome. The stripes of lace are beautiful. I'll go in and wash and then start around the block. I plan to eventually go three blocks in all directions. I will be well received.

*

Seventeen orders! People here don't know how to do it. They want to see my bobbin and how I weave it in and out of the threads. They are surprised it is made of a real bone, and which animal's? I show them the gold rivets, so small.

He squeezed me into the corner of the landing when I was on my way downstairs. I stepped this way and I stepped the other way, and then I knew he wasn't going to let me go past. He stretched his shiny lips wide and stuck his hand under my dress and clear between my legs so that I could feel myself *in* his hand, and he said, "Growing a beard yet, are ye?"

That's what he said. "Ye."

*

I push the chair over to the door and hook its top bar under the knob. I lie down on the bed (and this will never, ever, be *my* bed) and I look at the knob and try to be peaceful. I picture us all at home but it makes me too sad, like my heart is a giant bruise, so I dream about woods a little bit like our woods, where there are no people, only the animals. They move softly in the leaves, quiet and free, and I watch them from over here.

The knob stays still.

Why didn't I push him? Why didn't I push him down the stairs? Why didn't I run after him and stomp on his head and scream and bash him and cut off his fingers and his hands at the wrists, with a knife, with a knife from the kitchen?

*

I can erase him. Him and her where they are. My eyes make them grey and blur and then they're gone. At dinnertime – grey and then gone. I can do it without looking.

At the table, Aunt Nannie chews like it's work. My eyes tell her what her father did. What he said, "beard," and his hand so fast and his lips wet and shiny. *Your own father.*

Nannie stops with her knife and fork and looks down the table. "Be of a cheerful mind," she says. I harpoon her right in the heart.

*

What if I wear a dress like a night moth and float down this block? What if my feet lift right off the sidewalk, white and floating, and my pale skirt wafts out like wings and my arms all white and my fingers, my face, all white in the dark, and my hair undone and floating, my skin shining in the dark like nicotine flowers? And lightning bugs glimmering at the ends of my fingers, five on each hand, and two hovering at my ears, like thoughts of earrings?

I will be so beautiful to all the people on their porches.

BOILING

I need two hands to carry the boiling water from the stove to the sink. All the dishes – I need more hot water.

Everybody is gone somewhere, Uncle Murray back to work. The only ones left are me and Pepper, Felicity's new little dog. He is in my feet's way, bumping into my legs. Go! but he is only a puppy, he doesn't. The kettle is awfully heavy.

Don't do it!

And then I do – dribble boiling water on Pepper. He screams. Sorry! Sorry! He runs around the four walls of the kitchen and yips and yips. Sorry! I didn't mean to!

I did mean to.

I was outside of myself watching, and I did it on purpose.

Christine comes with peaches. Oh wonderful! But her eyes – dark, and dark underneath, like a sooty thumb wiped there and there.

Everybody home is fine. Eyes still terrible. Words in her eyes all through noon dinner, and I know she will tell me something.

We stand to clear. Aunt Nannie says, "Girls, I leave you to do up the dishes, as you will be wanting to visit," and she goes. In the kitchen, Christine holds me close two times more; we won't speak in here.

The backyard is good. We go to the very back where the rabbit is in his hutch on legs, Benjamin, big and heavy, bigger every day, his lovely soft fur. I take him out for Christine to hold and he is huge as a baby on her shoulder.

"Christine, what?" She puts Benjamin down, we lock him in.

"I had an operation. Dr. Thorne did it on my bed with a razor and Mama held a cloth with chloroform and it put me to sleep."

"What operation?"

"Down here," and she touches herself between her legs and she starts to cry. I can tell she's cried this cry a hundred times. I'm scared, and she cries, and cannot stop, and we lean against the tree and I try to hold her, and pry her hands away from her face, just a finger, but I can't – "Talk, Christine! Will you die? Do you have a disease?" I am turning fast the pages of Mama's Doctor Book in my mind, looking for pictures, and there aren't...I can't remember...there isn't a disease for down there.

"I don't have a disease. I had a clitor and now it's cut off."

"Why? Why is it cut off? What is it?"

"Juanita, down there, near where you pee, a tag. Mama says God left it by mistake, it's something left over we don't need. Like an appendix."

I know about an appendix. I look around and reach up my skirt and into my underpants. I quick think about him and his bony hand and fast in my thoughts I chop it off with the kitchen knife and it falls bloody on the grass and he staggers howling into the house, but what can he say to anybody in there?

"Do you feel it? Like a little dickie in front."

"Dickie? I can't find it."

"Just in the middle, and like a bud, like the bud of a flower. Not big like a lily's – smaller."

I can't find my clitor. "Christine, mine isn't here."

She hunkers down. I pull my pants lower. She moves my hairs to see better.

"Juanita, you don't have one."

"I don't have one?"

"I can't see it."

"Are you sure? Why don't I and you did?"

Christine sits back on her heels and looks stymied.

"I don't know about this. Did you have it cut off?"

"No!"

"Maybe when you were little?"

"Chris, I would know. We would all know. Christine, what about the others? Elizabeth? Ruth?"

"No, only me. Because I touched myself. I used to. Mama heard me sighing. Sighing and sighing, and she said to stop but I didn't, and she worried about me. She said we're here on God's earth, God's women, to use our brains and work and praise and have children. And the space down there is where the babies go in and where they come out and in between we're not to touch. It could make us very sick."

Mama never mentioned this to me. "Did it make you sick?"

"No. But Mama talked to Dr. Thorne. He said just to remove it and it won't be able to cause trouble. For her own good, he said, and Mama told me she prayed a long time and in the end she said *I consent*. At least, in her mind she did, but not in her heart, I could tell. She felt terrible."

"When was it?"

"The end of August."

"Christine, can I see?"

Christine is making herself small. "No."

"Christine, can you have babies?"

"I don't know. Yes. I bled so. I still hurt."

*

I find it. A tiny bud. It feels sweet, like Christine said. Like a butterfly giving me a thousand small kisses.

I feel dreamy...like a wild, itchy happiness...like water knees.

This terrible house goes away.

Did Mama do this? Before?

*

Christine is here again. She says it doesn't matter now and she's forgotten all about it. I shouldn't think about it either. All right. We walk down the block in the dark. Many lightning bugs.

I want to tell her about my new sweet feelings when I touch myself, but she looks at me too quick when I start, so I stop. Another darkness falls down in front of my eyes, named *Watch out*. It blots out Chris and the lightning bugs and the houses. If Mama found out, would she find someone to cut me? I would run, I wouldn't let her. Would Christine tell?

I am cold; I feel more lonely even than when I worked alone in the high field picking up falls.

"Christine," I reach out in the dark for her. I have too many thoughts. "Christine." Very bad.

She takes hold of my two arms with her two hands. I feel my muscles inside my sleeves because of her warm hands.

Now I can see; here is Christine, normal Christine.

For days, every thought is hopeless and bad. I think I will never see the world, I will never know all the things I want to find out. Then I feel too tired to care anyway; it's all stupid, I don't want anything, I don't want any place or –body.

I have one good thought: this badness will end.

*

Christine writes, Juanita, even if I got married and went away with my husband, we would still keep each other.

Married?

Some more: Juanita, why don't you write a letter to Mama? I think, What about? But what I'm really saying is I won't. How can I tell her she shouldn't have let Dr. Thorne do it. How could she? How can I feel the same about Mama now? I cannot. This feels like the end of the world.

Me dusting, and I jump when she comes into the hall. I have never seen this two-look on her face, and she is in a hurry. She is showing me something, and I do not understand: how to relax my muscles.

"In order that you may get a good night's sleep."

What?

"Lie down here. Now tighten your toes as much as you can. Now let go completely. Both feet. Now your knees. Tighten, let go, arms – every part – tight, let go. Do this before bed. A worthwhile activity. And put a smile on your face."

She leaves, and says before the door swings shut on her, "Your father wants you home for a visit. You'll take the train."

Oh. She wants Mama and Papa to see that I am thriving.

*

I will *not* take the corset home. But I will tell Mama about it. She will be almost scandalized. Amazed, anyway.

... God, as promised, proves
to be mercy clothed in light
— JANE KENYON, *Notes From The Other Side*

I have come home on the train.

"Hello, Papa."

"Juanita."

We stand apart, but our voices touch each other softly.

"Come; I've brought Mera."

"Papa! She's saddled!" (I'll sit up front somehow.) "Where is the wagon?"

"Your uncle needs it today. Come on up. Juanita, you have grown taller, maybe I should get in front."

Teasing! This is Papa saying *Sorry*.

Mera knows me (Of course!), she bumps my cheek. I bump her back and kiss her warm neck. She steps out dainty and sedate. Papa tells me the Hunters have started to unpack the everlasting spring, to haul the boulders away. They need the source. They have not said if they put the boulders there in the first place.

"Not yet," I say.

Papa says, "Never mind now. We will converse about chemistry." Why do I start to get tears in my eyes? Behind me, Papa is warm. Almost as warm as if I was leaning against him.

The air at the farm is full of breezes of sunshine and bees arcing. The yard out front is wider, more trees are cut down, their stumps still smoking. Mark and Elizabeth run to see me and shove each other, telling me things. Mama stands in the doorway and smiles at everybody.

*

I am looking at Papa across the table in the kitchen. He leans back, his hands palms up on the scrubbed wood, his fingers little pleadings. He seems to be looking at them, but he is not. He is moving words around in his mind to speak to me.

"Juanita, I lost my self-control. I knew that right away. Your Mama has helped me see I took out on you all the worries I had about other things."

I wonder what they are.

"I heaped all my fears on you; I was just like the Biblical Hebrews, piling their sin and fear on the back of a goat and driving it with stones into the desert to die."

Of course Papa didn't want me to die.

He knows my thoughts. "Juanita, I can see you are glad to see me. Thank you."

He has turned his hands over; he presses them into the table, he leans over to me. I cannot bear the unhappiness in his eyes. "It's all right, Papa."

"It was not, it is not."

His misery makes an emptiness between us. I move around the table and hunker down beside him. Better. Especially when he pats my shoulder. Then he smoothes my hair with his hand. Mama comes into the kitchen.

"Don't come in just now," she says to Mark in the doorway, and starts to scrape carrots.

"Papa, I am sorry I said 'I won't.'" Papa makes a groaning sound. Mama says, "You are both headstrong," and I think, "– and I am spine-strong."

*

"Mama, what was piling up for Papa?"

"Oh, so many things." As she hesitates, I think of them myself – how he works so hard to take care of us, how he wasn't raised to be a farmer, especially on land full of stones, how it was so hard to save Uncle Ed from bourbon.

"You don't remember Papa's Aunt Eudora. She was, even after all those years, so angry with Papa for leaving Locust Grove, that she disinherited him. That was hard because it showed that she had never forgiven him, but not hard because of her money, because your Aunt Carrie gave us half of her share. The hardest thing for Papa is your Grandma Mary Belle."

*

I don't know how to say this next thing, how to ask and talk to Mama about it. It's about how I left home. I wonder how else I would have. Mama would definitely have found a way for me to go away so I could go to school, just as she did for Christine. She would have ranged around in her mind for an old friend from when she went to Scarritt College, or when she lived in Webb City, someone who could use a young woman or girl to help in their home, and would take me in, in exchange for work.

I think I am gone from the farm forever. But I would have been anyway, even not standing up to Papa. My real, true life is over. Mama and Papa and George and Mark and Elizabeth and Ruth will never know my whole life anymore.

*

I didn't know I would do this, but here I am, looking; Papa must have been hugely strong, for the tear where the limb came off is more than an inch across. His face is a storm and he is lifting the branch high over his head and he will hit me.

*

Mama and Papa are in their room, studying and praying.

Another thing – I know it is no use, but I try to look it up, anyway, in the Doctor Book, what Aunt Nannie's father did. I don't know what to call it. The women's diseases section (this wasn't a disease) has thirty-eight pages: Menses, Tumours of the Womb, Ovarian Dropsy, Imperforate Hymen, more topics, but not what he did: a creepy man and Ye.

Twice I started to tell Mama, but then I didn't. She would think it was her fault, and there would never be enough prayers for that.

*

Page 1530 has a note on castration, which is mostly about Jewish law and men and "the removal of the prepuce." Nothing about a girl, about a clitor, although there is a short bit about spaying, which is about removing ovaries (girls and women only).

*

Maybe I should tell Mama about Uncle Murray, yes, I will. He comes home for midday meal, and afterwards, when the table is cleared, after I have washed and dried the dishes and put everything away, when everyone's gone off somewhere, he comes and bends over the sink.

He vomits his dinner. Then he washes his face and hands and the sink, and combs his hair with his hands. He puts on his cap and goes back to work.

Oh, I told her already.

moves its many hands
in our trees (oak, hazel, walnut,
pear)
– falls still.

Trees and wind know something
that lasts a long time.

It's the porches that give me the idea of going to Miss Craig's house, but I don't go over there until after it gets dark. Before that, I sit on my bed with my clothes on and watch the doorknob and stretch my ears.

I walk on the grass next to people's bushes so the streetlight on the corner will not shine on me. All the lights in Miss Craig's house are off. I walk quietly up her steps, which are cement and don't creak, and sit down in the corner of the porch farthest from the front door. I am still afraid, but it is better here. I listen to the crickets and a night bird for a long time and then, without knowing it, I fall asleep. When I wake up, it is almost light and I know where I am right away, but no one else in the world does, especially Mama. My plan is to knock on the screen door and not even say hello maybe, only, "Tell Mama where I am."

But I do not. I run down Miss Craig's porch steps and turn up the long block to Aunt Nannie's, where nobody will ask me about anything. I can't; I turn around and go back.

And here is Miss Virginia Craig from school looking surprised in her bathrobe, and she pulls me into her front hall and sits me down quick. "Tell me, Juanita." I tell about Aunt Nannie's father and she says, "This is important," and makes oatmeal for both of us. She lends me her comb for my hair and I wash my face and neck and my hands. We will walk to school to talk to the lady Dean.

There is no one at school yet, the hall feels quiet and huge. Only us: Miss Craig and me and now the lady Dean behind her door named Miss Grindlay in gold, and she behind her desk. She stands up as we come in and I think she is like Saint Peter, only not a man, only no beard, and with brown hair, and now I wonder why I thought of Saint Peter. "Hello, Juanita." She looks intently at me, and I feel Miss Craig beside me and I tell the story again, Ye and his wet lips and how I couldn't get away from his hand.

I am crying and crying, as if I am just a little thing who has got back home after being lost someplace. But I'm not home, I'm in Miss Grindlay's office. I don't even know her. I saw her nice face and started to howl.

"Miss Emack, do sit down," and she's come around her desk and she's handing me her handkerchief, tucking it into my hand; her fingers are warm and mean business. I spread it wide over both my eyes and keep blubbering.

Here behind my eyes I see Uncle Murray's face. He looks sad and tired and confused all at the same time. He realizes that I am going to leave his house, that I have come to find another place to live.

I think of Uncle Murray vomiting up his noonday meal every day before going back to work. He is sick and I know that he will die. In my heart I tell him I am sorry, I have to go, It's not you, and behind my eyes he fades away and I cannot tell if he understands.

Miss Grindlay knows something. "Miss Wyatt has told me about you; you are a favourite in her class. Of course, almost everyone feels like her favourite, but I think she has a special affection for you. Your living situation is difficult. Your aunt has quite a houseful, and she is a perfectionist."

I am glad Miss Grindlay speaks reasonably about Aunt Nannie, and I am surprised that she speaks so freely about another grown-up, but now I can tell she's thinking out loud to herself as much as she is telling me something.

"Can you find a place where they need a girl?"

I know the chances are maybe yes, maybe no, but right now I begin to feel a little as I did riding Roxie in Big Old Piney in the flood, my arms and legs full of Grandpa's determination, when I was sure we'd reach the other side, downstream maybe, but the other side just the same. There are three of us now, not only me.

"How can I speak to your mother?" And I tell her that Grandma Mirrill has a telephone; she will walk to our house.

"I will see to this, Juanita." I look at her. She looks sure too. Her eyes are hazel and she wears an oval gold pin right at the little dent at the bottom of her throat. Her face matches her voice – very good to be near, kind.

"Come to me after your classes. I will talk to your Uncle Murray and Aunt Nannie. With the approval of your parents, we will find you a good place to live."

*

I am moving to live with the Cosseys. As Mama says, "a new, a better start." To make a celebration of it, to commemorate my being older now, Mama gives me silver spoons. They once belonged to Papa's grandmother, my great-grandma, Margaret Turner (George Malcolm's Mama!). "There are stories to these spoons. Papa will tell you."

I hold them like a bouquet in my hands, and then one by one. All are thin with their great age, and this largest has been used to stir for a hundred years. Its stirring edge is curled and partly worn away.

Four of them are engraved in a lovely, flowing script, 'M.E.,' for Margaret Emack. The fifth is a mystery, engraved with an 'O.' Who is this 'O' person? Mama doesn't know, neither does Papa. George Malcolm knew.

I polish each one on my hem. I put each back in its flannel sleeve, roll the length of sleeves and tie the dark red ribbon.

That is how I have come to live with the Cosseys. They are very, very nice, I think. Mrs. Cossey is twenty-five, I am fifteen, their little girl is Margaret, and five. Ten years between us each way, and that is a good lucky coincidence that connects us right away. I can be useful, and I will be. Deciding this makes me feel strong.

Mrs. Cossey's father gives her money, so she gives me two dollars every week, on top of my room and board. This is riches, and oh! I need it. There are books, books to buy, and my fare to school, and shoes, and saving up. The thing is, all of a sudden Mrs. Cossey's father became a millionaire. He used to ride up and down the streets with his horse and wagon, selling coal oil for people's lamps, but a friend took him aside and told him to scrape up all the money he could, that gasoline would be his road to riches, everyone would be wanting an automobile, and automobiles require gasoline. So he sold the horse and wagon and opened three gas pumps in town – all the ones there are – and in no time at all he was a millionaire, with an automobile of his own. Mrs. Cossey is his pride and joy, he doesn't want her far away, so we live on the same block where she was raised, four houses down, and her father gives her all the money she wants.

And she, so nice, with a voice like singing. Not proud, not a slave-driver. Mr. Cossey too, who laughs a great deal in a jolly way that makes me jump. I have a room of my own, at the top of the stairs, on the right, with billowy white curtains at two tall windows.

I will miss Uncle Murray, and my heart hurts when I think of him missing me and vomiting in the sink after dinner every day. I will miss Felicity. Who will finish teaching her how to tat? I daren't go back to do that.

On Wednesday, after school, on top of saving me, Miss Craig bought four feet of my tatting. "The plain white will be suitable, and not too elaborate. Half an inch wide." Miss Virginia Craig, who went to study at Columbia University in New York when she was young. In the morning, she had read us *I Wandered Lonely As A Cloud* by William Wordsworth, and suggested we memorize it for today (Friday). I did, for I love it. I love daffodils. Tonight I will write a poem about Margaret and her father. The main thing to say about Margaret is she adores her Papa, whom she calls Daddy, which is their way in the Cossey family.

*

It isn't a poem. Instead, I just imagine.

Margaret is almost too big, but she is sitting under the table, her little house. She looks up at the rosy rafters and notices that four fluted columns hold the ceiling up. The smell of wood is maybe the first of all smells. All around her are legs and voices, and the best voice is the one that doesn't say much; she can hear its smile, and here are his legs, dressed in rough rusty-coloured wool. Here are his big brown shoes, his laces tied in double knots. He is His Majesty.

The Queen sits on the other side. She is laughing because of the people who came for supper and also the candles. Margaret thinks about laying her cheek on the silky legs, the little knitted stitches climbing up her mother's curvy legs, but she does not. The shoes of the Queen shine as dark as raccoon's eyes, their thin straps wind around her ankles and attach themselves to other straps with metal squares.

Margaret touches her own hair, she makes a circle with her fingers all around her head. She thinks, My crown of stars will feel like this.

One of my jobs is to take Margaret downtown on Saturdays to Tanner's store. We walk. She is young to be so concentrated on dishes, but she has a good imagination and pictures herself sitting at a table someday, pouring tea and passing cake and butter cookies on pretty plates and matching cups and saucers. I like her favourites – pink flowers on white with gold rims (real gold) and very thin. The thinness causes them to make a ringing sound when you put the cup on the saucer. In fact, it's that I like best: not, however, enough to save up for them as Margaret does. She told Mr. Tanner he had to save the dishes for her, until she has enough; she has over a dollar now. Mr. Tanner said she mustn't worry, they are open stock, which is puzzling, but seems to mean there are more if these run out. For the time being, Margaret daydreams and talks about them, and we visit Tanner's on Saturdays.

*

Two things to say.

Ella Renick died, of tuberculosis. She was away, sick, and we waited for her to come back to school, but she never did. We were all told at the same time; the principal made an announcement and said he deeply regretted giving us the news. Ella's sisters and brother would not be at school for a few days. I wonder what will happen to her books. Will her sisters want to wear her gym bloomers and other clothes? Are they full of germs? Is it important to burn her things? Will her mother keep them for remembrance, in a special drawer or a box?

When Carl Windel died a long time ago, Teeley told us that he lingered in the clearing for three days or maybe a week. After that, he entered the woods, where his spirit was at rest.

By now, Ella will be at the edge of town, walking through her grandpa's grassy field, toward the woodlot.

Many girls die of tuberculosis. May's older sister has it. They have put her in a closed room with no light. The doctor says she mustn't work her eyes, that it is possible he will have to bandage them. For weeks and weeks. Everyone says that there are not enough doctors for all the people falling ill. What this means I don't really know, because the girls die anyway.

*

No one here has encouraged me to pursue chemistry, just the opposite, and even though I get the best marks, my chemistry teacher never addresses me in a serious way, as he does the boys. He looks at me and sees Clever-Juanita-Who-Gets-Good-Marks, not Juanita who will become a chemist.

Miss Riddle says I must think about being a librarian, that I have the perfect disposition, and she would be proud to be my sponsor. This is nice of her, and maybe sensible, but wrong.

*

Two poems: one for Margaret for her birthday, and one I dedicate to Miss Craig who reads Emily Dickinson out loud to us.

A POEM FOR MARGARET, ON HER BIRTHDAY

I talked to a toad
darker than shadow
under the burdock
under the sill
I asked him the way
I could live in the winter
He answered me –
Still
Still.

I spoke to a toad
slick as new leather
who lives in the leaves
that grow under the step
I asked her to speak
of the sheen of her green–
ness, and quickly
she answered me –

Hop.

Emily, O Emily,
We made your black cake
It turned out wonderfully
As yours, black as a hole,
A slab like a hardwood mill-end,
Thick as meat.

We eat it
As if it is happiness,
We hear you whisper
In each inch and atom everyplace.

Perhaps I will explain to Miss Craig that we actually have not made
the cake yet, but I intend to make the suggestion to Mrs. Cossey. It
would be a beautiful Christmas cake.

I wrote this poem twice, the first time with quite a few dashes and a
lot of capital letters. "Black Cake," for instance. But that seemed as
if I was making fun of her, so I took them out.

LOVELY

Dear Nita,

You *will* have a white dress! One of the ladies at the rooming house doesn't need hers anymore and I took it apart. I am making it to fit me and it will fit you. I cut the skirt on the bias so it fits my stomach and my bottom smooth like a hug, and flares out wide when I walk. You will love it. The neckline is square, I couldn't change that, but it is lovely.

Love, Chris

*

Dear Christine,

Can you come for *Lady of the Lake?* Because the dress fits me *perfectly*, and one of the mothers bought tartan by the yard and fringed a large tartan square for each of us in the chorus, to wear over our white dresses, to be pinned on our right shoulder and draped across, front and back, and attached to our left waist.

It is Sir Walter Scott – with music! And at the Opera House. *We will be on stage downtown.* You have to come. All of us in white.

Lovingly, Juanita

*

In the mirror. Five feet five inches tall. Will I grow taller? And the dress is wonderful. Mama says - and it is true - Christine could stand on her head and cut out a dress.

My hair is almost black. I have braided it in a loose braid to hang down my back, and I would love my hair around my face to be smooth and shine like a blackbird's wing. It starts to, but it's May and humid already, and my side hair springs out curly. Shall I cut it?

Christine is coming! So is Mama, so is George!

*

This poem is about a memory:

PRAYERS

At night on our knees
Beside the bed
Now I Lay Me, then
When we are older
Mama prodding
You may add to that
And wondering
What?

*

Is God a long, handed-down story?

*

Mama writes me. She cautions me against the sin of pride, about being smart. She wants me not to forget that my brain is a gift from God, along with my body and my soul. I am to be humble about all three of them, and I think she means I am not to be stuck-up.

But it is me personally who feels wonderful when I win and am the smartest. This is such a good feeling that I do not want to stop it, like when I was the best runner at Pleasant Grove School.

I truly think it is all right to feel wonderful. I will talk to Mama about this, and tell her that I do not brag.

*

Dear Chris,

I bought a beautiful silver box, hinged. I say it's for carfare, that's what I will say to Mama, and she'll look at me sharply, and I'll carry on as if she hasn't and I'll say I need the carved silver roses and the carved silver leaves and the size of it just to fit my hand, and the bumps of the silver flowers nudging my palm. I imagine saying that.

The carfare and the streetcar: I hop on at Emerson Avenue, at the very end of the line, where the car has to turn around in a circle. The car turns in a big O under the hackberries and stops where I am, the first one on. I always get a seat, but first I open the small silver hasp and take out my ten-cent piece and drop it into the tall glass box where the coin falls this-way, that-way like falling downstairs. My box makes a small solid sound when I close it.

I love it, and I paid for it myself with money from tatting. I like to even think about using it.

I am not sleepy, and my work is done. I want you to hear me, Christine. Christine, don't get married.

By the time the car is halfway through town, the seats are all taken. I offer my seat to the same lady every day. She wears brown brown brown and always accepts my offer, and is nice. She works in the library at school.

Isn't it lucky Mama taught us good manners? Because this lady has offered me a job.

Love, Nita

When I wake up, the curtains are blowing hard, hard as loose sails on a clipper ship. A warm wind, and I hop out of bed and let it blow my nightgown too. My skin feels special.

Margaret knocks and comes in at the same minute. She has her hairbrush in her hand. We have started this, Margaret sitting on the side of my bed and me parked beside her, to brush out her wonderful brown hair and make it into braids. Most days she brings fresh ribbons (her mother is particular this way), but this morning she has brought yesterday's. They are the new favourites: grosgrain, and multi-striped.

We hear her mother's voice, from downstairs, and now closer, and now she's at the door and in. It's the telephone, for me, and it's Mama. And I am very surprised and Mrs. Cossey is trying not to look alarmed, and I gallop down the stairs.

"Mama!"

"I am at Annie's, Juanita."

Our house burned down. All night long last night, while our house was burning, I didn't know it. I just slept. This is queer and wrong, I should have dreamed it. Or waked up from a nightmare, feeling our house on fire and flying up like tall red tongues into the sky: falling, falling down.

Grandpa's uniform box is gone; it completely burned. Uncle Ed pulled Mama's chest of drawers and Grandpa's box with the letters inside – he pulled them out into the yard, and then the wind from the fire was too hot; he couldn't get back inside. The walls were roaring, he told Mama and Papa in Webb City, and he could hear the nails scream.

Grandpa's uniform and his sword – all, all burned. His two rows of buttons, up and down.

"Yes," says Mama, "metal burns."

Papa is heartbroken. Even though the uniform might have been full of moths by now, even though the sword was rusted, Papa is heartbroken.

I think of George Malcolm, my secret lover, my handsome man, full of adventures and raring to go. Today, even more than before, he is Papa's Papa. I give him back one more time.

*

Mr. Cossey says he'll make breakfast, but he stands on the linoleum looking as if he doesn't know where anything is.

What about Mera?

What about Roxie?

HOME

Home is best, everyone says
but what if the places you are
do not feel like home, and all your life you long
for the Other Place?

What if one day you're near to There,
your side in a stitch, a pitiful limp
under your sister's handed-down skirt
and that landscape says Not Here?

What if a wood of balsams
rushes into your nose?
You rip off your blouse and lie your bare skin
on the duffy forest floor
and beg to be let in
but you can't?

What if all your Home is Over There and No One
says I remember you?

SNOW

Quietness covers the world.
On Willer Avenue, snow
shines lilt-light on the lawn

has laid clean sleeves
on every limb and twig
as if the upper air declared
I'll do something beautiful
for Thursday.

A few men and women quietly
greet each other with their eyes.
At noon
the firetail of the sun quickens.
Silent, the sleeves fall down
and thicken the lawn.

PART FOUR

And did you get what
you wanted from life, even so?
I did.
And what did you want?
To call myself beloved, to feel myself
beloved on the earth.

— RAYMOND CARVER

Springfield High School Library, 1921

EMILY D. AND WALT W.

I have not given up on my good idea of becoming a chemist. I have taken every course I could. No one has encouraged me in the slightest, except that once, a long time ago, Papa's face lit up when I told him of my intention. But Papa had to stop being a chemist, and I stopped talking to him about it.

Mr. Cossey is on the Board of Trustees at Teacher's College at S.W. Missouri State. He is strongly in favour of my going there. I wouldn't have to pay. It feels like chemistry is slipping away, slipping away.

I am starting to wonder if my intention is fading. My disappointment, even. What I know is that I am submersed in poems because of Miss Craig. Listening to her reading poems out loud and talking about poets is like being transported by faith, growing wings. I get picked up and carried away, and I feel sure that the world of poetry is the true one. In class, everyone listens quietly, but afterward in the halls, on the way to History, so far as I can tell I am the only one who feels like this. Of course, it is hard to put these huge things into words. Maybe people would feel embarrassed to succeed.

I have the typewriter. It belongs to the Library, but I use it every day, as if it's mine. After I'm through at the Circulation desk, I come downstairs and here it is. I have not asked permission. After this semester, I am pretty good at typing, although I still look at the keys. I don't care! I love to see my poems looking so poem-like. I take them home in an old envelope addressed to Mr. Cossey. I try not to read them again right away because my opinion of them is too high; I'm still starry-eyed. It's better when I wait. Then things I've left out pop right out at me. Also, the things I shouldn't have put there in the first place.

Poems! (Not mine.) I keep getting new favourites. Am I fickle? But why should I pick one? Even two? I'll take a hundred. It would be wonderful to memorize all of them, to carry them around with me.

This week's treasures: Mr. Walt Whitman, especially "When Lilacs Last In The Dooryard Bloomed," a true, great cry of anguish about the assassination of Abraham Lincoln. "Out Of The Cradle, Endlessly Rocking," also "As I Ebb'd With The Ocean Of Life." There are so many I haven't read yet.

Listen to this:

This is thy hour O Soul, thy free flight into the wordless,
Away from books, away from art, the day erased, the lesson done,
Thee fully forth emerging, silent, gazing, pondering the themes
    thou lovest best,
Night, sleep, death, and the stars.

This poem does not apply to me at present; I am young. But maybe it would comfort Mama: "A Clear Midnight." No, I will not show it to her. She wants a lot more than stars. She wants Heaven after she dies, and she wants, right now, for God to let her know He can hear her. I still very much like Emily Dickinson, although I do not often know what she means, and Miss Craig says that sometimes she does not either.

Thank you, thank you, thank you, Miss Craig.

*

I have almost finished writing a long story, which I have kept a secret so far.

We are the lucky ones. We grow food – enough for the family and the darkies, and a lot to sell at the market in Washington. Griff takes fruit and vegetables and some poultry in the wagon, through the lines. Elbert is recognized in the city, and goes with Griff, to avoid his being harassed. We need money, the city needs food.

Everyone does; I suppose that is the way I can understand those who come in the night and steal. Griff and Jeremiah patrol the garden with dogs, keep watch in turns, and Elbert has joined them. I would go, on horseback as well, but he won't have it. The thieves are adolescent boys and women. We do not recognize them; they must be from miles away – perhaps as far as the Bay. They tether their horses at the edge of the near wood north.

*

Griff is badly hurt, beaten last night. Oriana is frantic and singing, *...like a motherless child.* We restored his dislocated shoulder, Elbert did, and he screamed. I mostly hovered, and ran to his house to get his wife and son. The terrible beating he received to his head and his chest and limbs will take weeks to heal. He fought, and told Elbert he was ashamed. Because he lost his stick. Griff, Griff.

Dora has shepherded everyone into the kitchen, and we pray. I ask her to read The Lord Is My Shepherd, and she does. *Surely goodness and mercy...*

I think of Dora long, long ago, and a day she taught me something that I haven't articulated until today.

That warm summer day – oh, it was *more* than warm – we were sweltering in the heat and humidity, a true Maryland summer day – I had kept the children in the house all day and then, as the sun was westering and filtering aslant through the trees, casting those long, mellow rays, I set them free.

They fled. Dora took off her pinafore, her dress, her petticoat and stockings. She shivered with pleasure as the air bathed her skin. I let her be. She wandered over the lawn and under the window where I stood inside. Maybe she was singing to herself, maybe she was lost in her imaginings. She sauntered in a slow, strolling pace, almost like a formal dance of a kind, maybe a pavane. I became lost in *her* being lost, she was that enchanting. She was caressing her tummy and thoughtfully feeling her navel with her fingertip. Again and again, and definitely singing now.

Dora saw me seeing her, and her face lit up with joy. Without words, she showed me her navel, so proud, as if to say Mama, look what I have!

True pride. The real thing, my Eudora.

The kitchen is hot and smoky; Lydia reads out loud to Oriana. She sounds out the words on the cover of Margaret's book:

The American Frugal Housewife
Dedicated to those who are not ashamed of economy
by Mrs. Child
"A fat kitchen maketh a lean will." Franklin Boston: Carter, Hendee, and Company, 1833.

Oriana is scandalized. She knows the punishment, and Lydia does too, and so does Mistress who is teaching, and doesn't she know they could all go to prison, and much, much worse for Lydia, a little darkie, reading?

"But this book has things for you, Oriana! Look – Apple Pi-e, Chicken Pi-e, Dandelions? What are Warts here for?"

Oriana turns her back and stirs.

*

Over the days, Lydia reads on. One day, Oriana says, "Read the chicken part." Lydia sounds the marks into sounds into words, words into sentences and instructions. Oriana asks, "How do you do it?" Lydia says, "These shapes sound like something. Say them out loud; that's reading." Oriana says, "Make Oriana."

Lydia does: OREANA. Oriana takes the scrap of paper, examines it as if it is a small interesting animal, and puts it in her pocket.

*

Lydia tells Margaret that Oriana can write her name now. Margaret is astonished and pleased, and briefly wonders if this is getting out of hand. She will tell Elbert later, not just now.

*

Margaret and her mother, Sarah Calder, will take several days in Baltimore, their Christmas treat. They will visit Kirk Jewellers and Silversmiths. Both women admire Kirk's craftsmanship with silver, and are especially fond of his dinner knives with carved-pear handles. Will the war have altered this joy?

Before she leaves, Margaret takes two large spoons from the kitchen drawer: Oriana's stirring spoons. At Margaret's request, Mr. Kirk will engrave a large 'O' on each handle.

The spoons were missed, of course. Oriana had looked everywhere, and in the end had had to report their disappearance to Master. When Margaret brought them back, she apologized to Oriana for the anxiety of it all, but urged, "Isn't it a *good* surprise? Your initial!"

*

I do not get out of bed each time, as I used to; Elbert does all that needs doing in the moment, and after daylight I will get hoecake and water from Oriana and take it to them. We do not say much to each other. Usually, they are exhausted, and, depending on how many there are, one will lie on the floor or they will sit tight in a row, to sleep. It's inhumane, but it's needed, and the best we have.

We never know how many there will be, but word has spread that we will take them in. Once we had to send two men away because the space was already full. When we close the panel at the side of the fireplace, no one can guess that there is an empty space there, inside.

I hear Elbert's calm, deep voice, but only the faintest sliding of shoes on the floor, and then the panel. Today, as always, they have come before dawn and they will leave tonight after dark. Some have come a very long way, walking by night, following the Drinking Gourd. Oriana used that term, and I realized it is the constellation we call the Big Dipper.

Elbert climbs back into bed. There are three: a mother, a father and a little boy. They have no exact destination, and no one to receive them there, but they are relieved to hear they are almost North. I will give them money, which I think they will have a dangerous time spending.

Oriana is in the kitchen, starting the stove.

I turn my ankle hurrying. Griff's son came to the door, panting, panicky. We are to come "Now, Suh," and we do, swiftly on the path to Griff's cabin. It is dark, and no moon to light us – no torch, we have come so quickly.

Griff is dead. Something inside, some deep injury, not healed, in spite of our efforts, Elbert's devotion.

We hear them from the moment we leave the side door: voices keening, moaning, a kind of low singing we know from other times, other dyings. Too late! Oh, too late, and Griff, it seems now – I never before felt it so – my dear friend. Come from my father soon after we came to Locust Grove. So long ago. Stop now; as long as you have not seen him, you cannot be sure.

The darkies stand as we come into the circle of firelight, stand and turn to us, we suddenly the centre of attention. We stop. There is quiet. Elbert speaks to Lydia, and she turns from him to her father, and her father bows his head a little and conducts us to the short step and the door, and now we are inside, and the women stand aside. Except for Griff's wife, who kneels, quiet as a chrysalis, beside his bed, and Griff is surely gone.

His face is calm.

I learn his sleeping face. An ache, such an ache. It's crazy, but *Griff, go find James.* Unexpected, and it's not seemly, I know as soon as I do it, and my ankle stabs, and I kneel beside Griff's wife, and now I remember – this woman who works each day in the fields – her name is Lallie. I am suddenly alarmed that she will stand and relinquish her kneeling to mine, but she does not; I stand.

Elbert puts his arm around my waist – to comfort me, to restrain me. I know him. Thank you, Elbert, you know me. I am ashamed to have drawn attention to myself, to have broken the holiness of Lallie's communion with her husband. Elbert tightens his hold on my waist.

Out in the middle of darkness, as if in the middle of the universe, the low singing sings on. The fire is small, but its sparks fly high. So high the stars have disappeared. My Lydia is over there, in the midst of the gathering of dark faces shining in the fiery radiance, her face hidden in her mother's smoky-coloured sleeve. Lydia is quietly sobbing. Her mother's face is very still. I do not know the song.

Jeremiah. That is Griff's son's name. He has two brothers and one sister, younger.

*

I take one of Mother's sheets from the spare cupboard, and slip out the side door, retrace my steps to the fire and Lydia there. "Take this to Lallie for Griff. I will wait."

Lydia comes back to me with Oriana, who says Lallie already has one; Griff already has one.

Springfield High School Library, 1921

GREAT-GRANDMOTHER MARGARET TURNER, SOMEDAY

I will give my daughter your two names
and six of your silver spoons
Mama and Papa gave me. Maybe

she will slip into the roomy sleeves
of your names when she becomes
the age you were
when James William and George Malcolm
cantered long the bright clay trace
from the house to the Baltimore Pike
to find Lee.

From the start
I loved the spoons – so thin
with use at your house
that they bend if we're not careful. One,
the biggest, must have stirred for years, the edge
is worn and curls up as a leaf does,
growing old. I know
that he did not, James William, he
was shot and died in Virginia. *A mistake!*
wrote his brother home. *His goodness*
should have saved him.

Margaret Turner, where did you keep
George Malcolm's letter home? Where put God
you'd trusted all your life
until then?

Did you unpack Him from that place? Dutifully
scrub His face and hands with prayers
and dress Him in an altered,
less resplendent
suit of clothes?

*

Maybe she couldn't do it. Maybe she was so terribly shaken that she lost her faith – That Faith, not faith in Elbert and her parents and the horses. And her children.

That would be so very sad and heartbroken all over again. Mama was. Mama lost her faith: Mama, after the little stillborns, after asking the little ghosts for forgiveness not because they couldn't live – that wasn't Mama's fault – but because she was relieved they didn't, we so poor and so many of us. She asked God every day and every night and He turned His face away.

*

How can I believe in such a Person?

*

(The spoons are plain, and have a lovely soft shine. Each except one is engraved 'M. E.,' flowing on the handle. How beautiful! The sixth, the biggest, has an 'O.'

Who is 'O'?

"Juanita, we do not know. And we have tried.")

*

I had a dream in the night that I must carry a message to Mama, if she won't think it too unbelievable. Well, I will carry it – that everybody is saved. The dream is full of colour – a wide meadow, but that does not tell the whole of how everything looks and is. Everything is saturated through with light, as if every one and every thing is transparent with golden light shining through, except we are not actually transparent; we are ourselves, solid. Maybe the light is *inside* all of us, shining through. We are ourselves, fleshy and leafy and grassy, full of light.

I know this in the dream: the world is exactly as it should be. We don't need at all to hurry, or to force. It is easy here; we need never be afraid.

*

Someone smiles at me in the halls. A boy. Who is handsome.

How very strange it is that our daffodils leap and bow all around the house, all over our hill, while the world is being torn to tatters.

General Lee was defeated at Petersburg. His line, in the end, thinned to but one soldier every twenty feet. George's Company joined in the last cavalry assault, but it was for naught. So it is told, but we do not know it from him. We do not know where he is at present. Lee's poor broken army marched west from there. They were starving, and food was promised them at Appomattox. But the supplies were not delivered.

We can imagine, then, that Lee took a long, sorrowful look at the exhausted remnant of his Northern Virginia Army and thanked them – that they were still willing to fight on: told them that he would surrender them.

He did so, on their behalf, to General Grant, at the McLean home. The two sat at separate tables in the sitting room. Each man signed the document of surrender. Lee was impeccably dressed in his dress uniform, his engraved sword at his side. Grant wore soiled boots and a private's red shirt. We do not believe this was a mark of disrespect, but a mark of the hurried nature of their meeting. They say that Grant was deeply touched by Lee and his men.

Lee mounted Traveler – everyone knows his horse – and rode away. His men remained and were fed. Were they taken prisoner? I suppose so, but perhaps not. We yearn for news of George. We never become accustomed to the silences. But I expect the war will be over soon. A blessing and not.

Two days since, Good Friday, Mr. Lincoln was shot in the back of his head by a Mr. John Wilkes Booth, who is an actor here. Lincoln died yesterday morning in a boarding house where soldiers had taken him, very near the Ford Theatre, where the shooting took place. His son, Robert, was by his bedside as he died, but Mrs. Lincoln was not; she had been taken away, for she was hysterical and lost control of herself, poor, desperate woman.

Booth had come into the Presidential box only a few feet above the stage, with a pistol and a knife. He shot Mr. Lincoln at that close range, then jumped down onto the stage. There are rumours that he had been drinking. Then he fled backstage and out. We know that stage, we know that very box.

It had been advertised on broadsides all over the city that the President would attend that particular performance. "Our American Cousin." With the distinguished Miss Laura Keene.

*

The streets of Washington are teeming with crowds of darkies, weeping and crying aloud. Here, our own people are circumspect; they, I am sure, have greatly mixed thoughts. As do we; we feel complicated and at odds with ourselves about Lincoln. He was a good man and a brave man; he laboured with his very life's breath to keep us united. *And*, he was undeniably our enemy, no matter his words at his inauguration, he was the chief of the forces aligned viciously against us. We cannot forget the atrocities, the murders, the brutality. But our hands, too, are greatly soiled. Can God forgive us?

Throughout all these territories controlled by the Union, and that of course includes us, there is almost an hysteria, as everywhere troops hunt down Lincoln's assassin, and others (apparently there were others) who were, or might be, part of the conspiracy to kill him.

We know the Union slogan, "Come Retribution."

We must be careful.

Mr. Seward, too, was attacked. He was severely stabbed, but he lives.

We know that George is acquainted with Booth.

We must leave home. Not far – only to Baltimore; we reassure ourselves as best we can that it is safe to do so. I will stay on with Mother and Father, and Elbert will stay the night and return early in the morning. Father is ill; he collapsed. It is his heart. Oh, Father, we have counted on you always to be the most robust of us all!

He is abed and calm. He smiles, consoles us. "My affairs are in order." Mother cannot bear it. "How can you say so? With this war and its undoubted outcome? Order! Whatever may that mean in the dreadful chaos of these days? Our very livelihood. You, my dear, my Sir, you are to recover!" Her passion will surely see to it.

*

Elbert and I come home together in the morning. Jeremiah rode after dark last night, came to get us.

Within three hours of our leaving yesterday, a detail of Union soldiers came to the house, looking for George. They slashed all our beds again, they tore the curtains down and left our furniture unmoored. They splashed hot food and broken crockery on the kitchen floor. Of course they did not find him. George would never have endangered us by coming home in these fraught days, hours after Mr. Lincoln's death.

But George has been under suspicion for years.

*

We had left Eudora to look after her brothers in our absence. When the soldiers came to the front door, she shooshed the young ones into the kitchen to Oriana and barred the soldiers in the front hall. She relented, but against her will.

After their search and not finding George, the young soldier in charge could think of nothing to do but arrest Eudora. Eudora refused to go. "I am responsible for my brothers and I will not go with you."

Now that it is all over and all the family is safe, I admit it amuses me to picture the dilemma of the young man, caught between two strong-minded individuals: his commanding officer out there someplace, and our daughter.

He and his men retreated to the porch, then about-faced back and into the kitchen, where he wrestled Oriana out of his way. They rounded up the children, Eudora too, and marched them to the porch, herding everybody toward the lane.

Asa Stabler – wonderful neighbour! He told us later that he had seen the detail marching up the lane, single file, to the house. He knew that Elbert and I had gone to Baltimore. He hesitated some, then galloped up our lane and intercepted the whole proceedings. Two things about Asa Stabler: he is a Quaker and a pacifist, and he is a well known Union man. He told the soldiers they must release these children, that under no circumstance did they represent a threat to the Union. The soldiers did so.

When we get home, the boys are in high spirits, tell us the tale, all the details ("Father! Soldiers! Rifles!") and yet more details. (Frank says one of the soldiers walked through the rooms of our house, saw the destruction wrought, and looked scared.) I send them out of doors. They rustle up long sticks and parade about the lawn, issuing orders. Ned too – only six, and already loving being a soldier.

Later, Eudora tells it all from the beginning. She weeps. It is mostly from relief; I am grateful for that. When she leaves my arms, and all the afternoon, I see in her a particular inwardness that was not there before. Perhaps she feels more womanly; it seems so. It is in part that she wears a handed-down dress that I gave her, but mostly it is something else.

We are told that George's Company did not surrender. On the day that Mr. Lincoln died, they moved away to Lynchburg, where the Virginia State Government has moved for safety: moved by train, each car marked "Treasury Department," "War Department," and so on. Mr. Jefferson Davis was on that same train, and his Cabinet, travelling from Richmond - now burned to the ground - to Lynchburg.

George's Company has moved into the Shenandoah Valley. General Lee has advised the Confederate States Army to disband.

*

After all, after all, many of them just ride home, in twos and threes. They do not surrender. George is not among them. We hear that he rides the countryside, gathering men together, and horses. He is forming a new Company.

*

Elbert writes letters. All the length of this war, Elbert has written letters.

Mary Rose Brown is having a party on Saturday, a Saint Patrick's Day party, maybe; anyway, it is on St. Patrick's Day, and Mama and Papa will be getting ready to plant potatoes. Papa says it's easier to plough now, because Old Kate is not as obstreperous as she used to be and that is a good thing because I (Papa) am not as strong as I used to be. He is wrong about that last part; he hasn't changed at all. When I think about Papa growing old, I want to fly back to the farm and stay there. I will not, but the ache in my chest says that's what I will.

Burniss has invited me to go with him. Burniss is a Meador, and we are probably related. His family comes from around Noel, and so does Mama's. Also, there's a professor of History and Economics at Drury College in town who is a Meador. He is a genius, everybody says.

So I said Yes, thank you, Burniss. For one reason: he is so nice, and for another, I don't have another plan for Saturday, and a person cannot say No for no reason. However, I do have a reason, but it is confusing. Burniss and Helen Sparks have been sweethearts all through high school and even before. Why doesn't he ask her? Maybe something happened to their devotion. Anyway, here we go; Burniss will pick me up and we'll walk over.

I wish I had a handsome coat to wear over my *Lady of the Lake* dress.

Mr. Cossey gets excited when Burniss comes to the door. He acts hugely surprised, as if I hadn't mentioned this would happen. Did he forget? He embarks upon a barrage of questions about Burniss's father and mother and where they live and what are his plans for the rest of his life. I feel a little embarrassed, but I can count on Burniss;

he looks composed, and speaks in calm sentences.

We walk to Mary Rose's house. It is probably her mother who has attached green paper elves and shamrocks to their front door. The door suddenly opens even before we knock and two little boys tumble out – Mary Rose's little brothers, they must be, and they hurry us into the house, into the hall, and we are officially at the party. They run off, hollering for their sister. Who comes to meet us, and here is someone else. The someone else is the handsome boy who smiles at me at school between classes. "Walter," says Burniss, and the handsome boy is named Walter. When I look at him – the strangest thing – I wish I hadn't cut my hair. Burniss is saying, "Juanita, I'd like you to meet Walter Thompson," and he says, "Walter, this is Juanita Emack," and I can tell that everybody here, in this very moment, knows that I am Juanita Emack.

That's about all I hear of words. But this beautiful face gives me a smile. It is the sweetest smile I have ever seen. Just like that, and a little nod, looking at me all the while, and smiling, and I must have said Hello, but I don't remember holding out my hand or saying anything myself. And Burniss says, "Now, Juanita, I will take you home." And I am almost as surprised as I was when he invited me in the first place, and maybe we say goodbye to Mary Rose Brown and her parents, but I don't remember it, and we walk to Cosseys, me seeing the sweet smile all the way.

*

Helen Sparks asks me on Monday if I liked Walter, and I find out then that Burniss went to pick her up after he took me home, and they'd gone back to the party, and Walter, she said, felt terrific because at last he and I had been introduced.

*

He walks with his hands in his pants pockets. He thinks about things, walking along, and even when he's not smiling at someone, there's a smile-smoothness on his face (and his lips are so very rosy and red). His favourite subject is History. He thinks about his music too, his clarinet. He plays in the Boy Scout Band; they will go to St. Louis to play at a Jamboree.

These days he is teaching his big brother, John Ward, how to shave. John Ward is very big, with a big echoing voice, and I am a little afraid of him, but Walter says Don't be. He is only two or three years old so far as being grown up is concerned, and affectionate, and wants to hug and kiss even though he's so big, but Don't be afraid, says Walter; it will confuse him and maybe make him cry, so I try.

After school, Walter works at the Mechanical Shops for the 'Frisco Railroad. His father is the Boss there. Royal Stevenson and Brisbane Hanks work there too – full time. Walter loves them; they laugh and joke and look out for each other. They all look out for each other, it seems.

Walter has another brother, younger, who is normal, and in love with a prissy girl named May. Also, two sisters, and his mother, who is Alice and so, so nice, and has another baby on the way.

We go see *A Midsummer Night's Dream*, and he gives me a box of Whitman's Sampler chocolates, in a brass box with a Turkish woman on the cover. We eat most of them, but agree to save some for Margaret.

I have melting feelings over my whole body.

I have brought them with me. I take Oriana's spoons from the flannel roll; I run my thumb over their thinness and the tattered edges, worn from all her scraping and stirring. In her kitchen, she is humming *a long way from my home*, and now she asks Lydia to read again *Pack your butter in a clean, scalded firkin, cover it with strong brine, and spread a cloth all over the top, and it will keep good until the Jews get into Grand Isle*. What could that mean?

*

I had to know them. It was not difficult to start, for I had the actual letters-home from James William and George Malcolm, I had held in my hands, when I was a child, the worn grey wool of George's war coat. Papa had me read the newspaper accounts in his possession. It was worthwhile work, and so interesting, to fill in some spaces, some of the teeming everyday and extraordinary life lived between this letter, that report, that photograph. I had to restore Grandpa's sword and his Officer-of-the-day sash. Bring him back. To his mother and father, to Papa.

I needed to know that they were not as poor as us, that they were full of normalcy and goodness, even though they owned human beings. Even, that they killed. I had to make up a story about how the biggest spoon came to be engraved with 'O.'

I didn't set out to make George Malcolm more true-to-life so I would not be romantic about him anymore. But that happened. I began to love his mother, Margaret Turner, and as that happened, I came to love him more as she did, devotedly and a little impatiently.

Now I love Walter with all my heart. Will I tell him about Grandpa being my dream-lover? Long, long ago? And my spine and his? Yes, I will; I will tell him *everything*. Mama, Papa, Christine, all of us. I will bake him a coconut cake for all his birthdays in all the Januarys.

*

I miss Locust Grove very much, already. Especially Margaret Turner. Oriana. And Lydia. "Mars" Ned is so adorable, running everywhere, tow-headed little boy. Griff.

*

I lift the cover from the typewriter.

I will follow with a "farewell" section, Margaret Turner to Juanita. Maybe I will have her pick up her photograph from the cherry sideboard (looking like Emily D.) She will think about the girls and women who will come after her, what they will see when they look into her receiving eyes. "I hope it will not be lost," is her worry about the photograph. And about herself – "Will they see that I was a serious person and a fine horsewoman, that I drove Elbert to distraction at times, and loved him to distraction always. As well as our children, and all my household. I forgot how to laugh partway through the war, but someday I'll remember how again."

It is in my power to tell her that the photograph was lost, but I will not. But I am sure, just as I had her surmise, that she and Emily D. could have been sisters, so alike did they look. I could recite for her Emily's poem, which she could never have known:

> I'm Nobody! Who are you?
> Are you – Nobody – Too?
> Then there's a pair of us!
> Don't tell! they'd advertise
> – you know!
>
> How dreary – to be – Somebody!

How public – like a Frog –
To tell one's name – the livelong June
To an admiring Bog!

She would adore it.

EPILOGUE

As badges of lichen are patient
their slow lace

as old ice
creeps north

and slow as Heron lifts
the burden of her body into Air

Mom lies floating between wakefulness and sleep. It comes to her that the soil of America was saturated with sorrow from early on. The timeless wheel that brings all things around was broken: too many buffalo slaughtered, Sioux and Shoshone murdered, terrifying deaths from diseases come from Away, so many children and mothers and fathers smothered in the holds of ships, so many torn from each other on the selling block. Not to this day has all that been properly mourned.

"No one won, no one conquered. We all step upon the land every day and the grief seeps up into us, every one. There was always a sadness in Papa, underneath the jokes, his teasing ways, his workaday intentions and his stubbornness. Not that he ever spoke of it. Certainly he would be astonished to know anybody thought he was a sad man. Think of his long embeddedness in the lovely, hurt fields and hills: Maryland, Kentucky, Tennessee, Louisiana – in his own lifetime, and through the long body of our family, in America since 1634 when The Ark and The Dove landed at St. Mary's City on Chesapeake Bay."

Mom is thinking out loud, as if she is writing it down, down so everyone after her will think about these things.

"If I had been bold enough, and if Papa had been more given to that kind of self-knowing, I might have asked him (but I was too young and distracted to notice), and he might have confided, that the sadness that was always there began before he was born, when his own father served in the Army of the Confederacy, when his father's beloved brother died at Chancellorsville."

"Richmond was bad. Grandpa's brother was there also, and in a letter home to their mother, wrote, 'the city is filled with the wounded...it is horrible to behold.' Libby prison overflowed with soldiers of the army of the Potomac, more than ten thousand in the end, and James wrote, 'I have seen a number of them when they were brought in and could scarcely help pitty, they were so humble and obedient.' James William died at Chancellorsville in '63. It was only a day after he (with only four men!) captured a Pennsylvania regiment: a surprise, a mistake, really – James's bluff. He'd stumbled upon them in the woods and, thinking fast, challenged them to throw down their guns or they'd be blown to kingdom come, every last man. When it was done, it was for Grandpa to go home to his heartbroken mother and father.

"There was no winning that war; Lee acknowledged his fault after the slaughter at Gettysburg. And think of what it had been like for him! He hadn't wanted Virginia to secede, his home, and when it did, and when Lincoln asked him to be the Union general, he couldn't; he went to the South, but he thought from the start it was going to be a waste. There were not enough men in all of the South to win. No gunboats in the James River to back the few. Everywhere, everywhere, the land lay in pieces, soaked and heavy with blood. And James William dead."

"I knew only some of these details when I was young. The letters home from George Malcolm and James stayed in a wooden box in Mama and Papa's room. Uncle Ed rescued them when our house burned down. When I grew up, I burned two of them that I thought would shame the family. *I am ashamed of that.* They told the story of George Malcolm after the war. Unable to accept defeat and Lee's surrender, he rode hard over miles of the South, gathering men. He formed a regiment of men of like mind – they would fight on – with more reason to keep fighting than capacity to surrender.

"I think often about George Malcolm, who he was, what he lived, and I think, 'Papa was made of this.' And, 'We children lived in the midst of this, and we didn't know.'"

*

When she woke up in her bed on the Wednesday before the Saturday she died, Juanita took note that she felt completely rested. Her legs lay deeply relaxed. Her head and neck, especially, had surrendered to gravity and the pillow, and her face felt smooth, as if she had been out in the rain.

The dream shows itself to her again. She and her mother, Mallie, are walking together. How wonderful that they are the same age! Like sisters – maybe even twins, their long white hair pinned up, in pale cotton dresses to their ankles. Juanita is surprised to see she is more bent than Mallie, and straightens. It is easy. The feeling of collapse is completely gone. She is light and light-stepping.

They are at the farm at Elk Creek, down where the first house was, before it burned. The grass is alive with jumping, winged creatures – brilliant green grasshoppers and underneath, audible as it would never be in waking, the tissue-paper sound of a snake winding.

The two speak to each other without words. Juanita tells her mother that the evening before she had been so very weak and dozy, and hadn't known how she would manage to get herself to bed. That she had nevertheless slotted into her machine the CNIB tape of an Englishman reading Plato's *Symposium*. Even as she did it, she thought to herself she would surely never be capable of concentrating, tired as she was, and her thinking so short-circuited, but to her surprise, "Mama, I got interested!"

Mallie hears all this. And while she is listening, her eyes are casting about in the grass, looking for something. Juanita thinks, She's looking for a plant. A wildling, like we both like. Maybe Sweetherb.

"Mama, I loved his logic, the clarity of his argument. It was wonderful. And then – I've never done such a thing, Mama – it was so unexpected. When Socrates took the hemlock and drank it, I cried."

Now they see it. The animal is only a head: large, brown, with fur on its face soft and glossy as silk velvet. Its nostrils are enormous, and the brown of the fine nose-skin shades to pink entering into those big holes. The eyes are fringed around with long lashes and shine. Is it a bison?

The silken grass parts. Now they see that the whole of the immense creature lies on its side. The head has been severed, but it is fitted to the body as if re-attached, and the only signs are the distinct line of a break in the hide, which wells and flows dark red, and a widening pool of deep red all around in the grass.

Mallie and Juanita hunker down, knees so flexible, as if they are girls, and watch. The animal breathes and breathes, and the warm breath plays on their knees. Watch, says the creature, and they do. Small at first and slow, then more assertively, rapidly, bright sprouts emerge from the giant ear, lengthen. Barley. It is barley. The shoots crowd out fresh and green. They thicken, until the whole of that benign face is obscured. The animal's whole head a waving bouquet of barley.

She woke up rested. She had the thought that a person could always be grateful, rested like this.

Later in the morning, she had the further thought that Mama, on the long, grassy slope down to the creek, got what she thought she never would, got saved.

*

So alive did her dream remain that, in the afternoon, she added to it. Mallie and she look up from the waving bouquet of fresh, healthy barley. The glance between them is of utter understanding, and now they see another figure: Teeley, standing there, her hands clasped before her. She has been here all along. Another figure – a slender woman, her smooth brown hair pulled back, revealing her high, smooth brow. She wears a dark ribbon around her neck, with something shiny pinned in front, and a tea-coloured lace collar on a long, brown gown. She looks like Emily Dickinson, except the breast of her gown has a deep stain from a terrible wound. I know who she is, and so does Mama. We all feel the strong heartbeat of the animal through the bottoms of our shoes.

*

Wichita, Kansas – August 5, 1904
London, Ontario – July 14, 2006

*

Of course, there is always more.

*

We waited five years. Walter's mother would not sign permission for him to marry before he turned twenty-one, so we had to wait. I got a scholarship to go to Library School at Ann Arbor. It wasn't called the University of Michigan in those days – maybe not very much even now – but that's what it was; everyone called it Ann Arbor. Isn't it a romantic name? I was excited to go, and went even before I finished my undergraduate degree at Drury. To finish it off, in Ann Arbor, I studied German, of all things. All I really remember today is "Sah ein knabe ein röslein rot." I'll sing it. German, along with my library studies. A nice young man coached me, and he fell in love with me. He asked me to marry him. I considered it, can you imagine that? For a time, Daddy seemed far away.

I am grateful I had the intelligence to telephone Walter to tell him. He was at home. He told me to give him the number of where I was, and to stay exactly there, and he would call me back right away.

He called from the train station. He told me I could not marry anybody else. He loved me and I was to marry him and nobody else. He was crying.

It was the end of term. I was finished my studies, Walter was too; we would meet at the train station in St. Louis and get married there. That's what we did. Walter's mother knew a minister there, and he married us and his wife was our witness, and I did not wear the beautiful silk and lace I'd sewn; I wore my travelling dress – pink wool. Because it was raining. Still, it was pink kasha wool. Daddy gave me the platinum ring with tiny diamonds all around.

We went home to our families, so everyone could be glad for us. Mama (can you imagine?) had formal announcements engraved, to tell the world we were married.

We moved to Cambridge. Walter had a choice between Harvard and joining a Wall Street firm, like his best friend, Bert Goss. He consulted with Dr. Meador at Drury, who told him, "*Nobody* should turn down Harvard." I got a library job at MIT. We moved into a tiny apartment next to the Hasty Pudding Club. As soon as we could, we bought a Dodge touring car. We kept pennies in a jar, Walter played squash with new friends. Papa wrote to say we certainly should visit our Maryland cousins on our way home at the end of term, before picking up George at Bible College in Tennessee. That was, of course, well before George became a Mormon.

*

It was a joyful meeting in Maryland. Walter and I had all our worldly goods – not so many – in the back seat of the Dodge, and we drove up the long lane to Locust Grove, where Papa's father was raised. Now the farm belongs to Grandpa's baby brother, Ned, and his wife, Edith Lura French of Cleveland. Their daughter, Ellen, is seven years older than I am. Edith met us at the front door, "You come from a *wonderful* family!" Walter and I intended to stay for an afternoon, but were held captive for two weeks. George, waiting in Tennessee, was beside himself.

I told Aunt Edith about the silver spoons that Mama gave me, that had come from this house. She led me to the sideboard and opened the top left drawer.

"These spoons have been kept here since before Ned was born. They were Margaret's. I knew her well, but as the years go by, this house tells me more and more about her. She was a wonderful woman, and dearly loved."

The spoons are identical to mine. They are engraved with the same flowing 'M.E.,' except for one. It is engraved with a large 'O.'

"Edith, who is 'O'?"

"No one has been able to guess, and we have tried."

"I..." I quickly closed my mouth.

*

Walter and I had been put in the bedroom with the pistol in a thick brown leather holster on the bedpost. Walter was pulling off his socks.

"I almost told Edith that I knew, I almost said that Margaret kidnapped Oriana's stirring spoons and took them to Kirk's in Baltimore to have them engraved. For a minute – O less than that – I forgot that I made it all up, on the school typewriter. So I stopped myself. Edith closed the drawer and we walked away from the spoons. Walter, say something."

"Who's to say? Maybe the story happened just like you said."

*

Just before I left Ann Arbor on the train, to meet and marry Walter, Miss McClench, who was my boss at MIT, gave me a tea party. Little cakes and sandwiches, and a silver bowl – filled with blue lupines!

My dear Dora,

Yours of the third instant has just been received. I regret exceedingly to learn the death of Uncle Harris, though it was by no means unexpected. From your previous letters I supposed it impossible for him to recover. How dreadfully his loss will be felt by the whole family. What will Aunt Rennie do without him? I am distressed to think of the sad bereavement, yet such is the lot of us all.

What is the little affair you have on hand? I am anxious to know. I do not know that I ever heard of a Mr. N.T. Davenport, though the latter name is quite familiar.

The party Miss Low mentioned was Captain Fred Smith. He called on me before leaving the city, and desired to see you, whereupon I gave him your address. He was married to a niece of General Breckenridge last year, and left her in New York while he went to Texas. This looks rather strange to me, and until I find out the cause and truth, I would not desire you to encourage his visiting you. I am inclined to think he is a rather light character. Any man who will ill-treat a lady or speak lightly of them, lowers himself in my estimation. I do not wish you to allude to this to anyone for the report may be incorrect.

Cousin Fannie's *beau*, Captain Maddox, I did not know. If he is the same party whom the Yankees arrested the first year after the war, and who was afterward in the employ of the Confederate states as a blockade runner, he is a man of no character whatever. He lives in St. Mary's County.

I am glad to learn John is having a pleasant time in Montgomery Co., and that he and Frank are both going to school again.

When you write home, give my love to Father and Mother. It has been a very long time since I have heard from Mother. Her letters will be anxiously looked for.

New Orleans is beginning to resume its usual gayety, as the cool weather approaches. Business is quite active and the City is growing rapidly every day. I would like very much to have you and Mother make me a visit this winter.

I have a great many very warm friends here who ask after you very frequently, and promise, if you visit New Orleans, to make your stay delightful.

In the course of a few years, if my prospects continue as bright as they now are, I will have a home of my own here, and then will insist on you living with me.

Give my love to Aunts R., E., M., and Grandma. A kiss to Cousin Fannie.

Goodbye,

Yours devotedly, George

FOR THEIR BENEFICENCE

My ardent thanks to these kin and collaborators, who told the
stories and polished the spoons:

Margaret Turner   Eudora Virginia   Maria Malvina
Edith Lura French   Ellen Phelps   Juanita's sisters Elizabeth
and Christine

A faithful cohort of friends has kept company with *Juanita Wildrose*
over these years; I am exceedingly grateful to each of you. When you
have added up your contributions, multiply by ten – minimum.

Alice   Ana   Anne   Dennis   Douglas   Joanne   John   Molly
Nancy   Stan   Thelma   Tiff   Valerie

Thank you, Beth Follett, for your peaceful voice and steady
guidance, and for welcoming *Juanita* into your home.

Charlie, you are a true friend to both of us.

Especially, Thank you, Mom.

ACKNOWLEDGEMENTS

The chapter entitled PLEASE READ THE LETTER is an extract from "War of the Rebellion," official record of the Union and Confederate Armies.

Lines in the chapter entitled LOVE are from Walt Whitman's poem, "Out Of The Cradle, Endlessly Rocking," from the 1861 edition of *Leaves of Grass* (Thayer & Eldridge, Boston).

"A Clear Midnight," by Walt Whitman, first appeared in a circa 1900 edition of *Leaves of Grass*, published by David McKay, Philadelphia.

Emily Dickinson's "I'm Nobody! Who Are You" appears, memorably, beautifully, in *My Letter To The World And Other Poems*, with illustrations by Isabelle Arsenault (KCP Poetry, 2008).

The American Frugal Housewife, by Mrs. Child, twelfth edition, Boston: Carter, Hendee & Co., 1833.

All photographs, sketches and letters are from the Estate of Juanita Emack Thompson, with the exception of the 1987 photograph of Walter & Juanita, taken in Bayfield, Ontario, by their son, John Marcus, and included here on page 287 with kind permission.

PHOTOS ON PAGE 103, clockwise from upper left: Officers at Libby Prison, Richmond, Virginia, Lt. George Malcolm Emack, seated right; George Malcolm Emack; Locust Grove, Beltsville, Maryland.

THE AUTHOR
Susan Downe lives in London, Ontario.
She studied English and Philosophy
as an undergraduate, at age forty she
studied Gestalt theory and practice,
and psychoanalysis, and practised in
these fields for sixteen years. She is the
daughter of a woman named Juanita
Wildrose.